Bittersweet

Bittersweet

DREW LAMM

CLARION BOOKS
New York

Clarion Books
a Houghton Mifflin Company imprint
215 Park Avenue South, New York, NY 10003
Copyright © 2003 by Drew Lamm

The text was set in 13-point Adobe Garamond.

www.houghtonmifflinbooks.com

Printed in U.S.A.

Library of Congress Cataloging-in-Publication Data

Lamm, C. Drew.
Bittersweet / by Drew Lamm.
p. cm.
Summary: When her beloved grandmother suffers a stroke, high school junior
and talented artist Taylor finds her inspiration and creative energy disappearing until she learns to reconnect with others and herself in unexpected ways.
ISBN 0-618-16443-X
[1. Grandmothers—Fiction. 2. Grief—Fiction. 3. Interpersonal
relations—Fiction. 4. Artists—Fiction.] I. Title.
PZ7.L1817Bi 2003
[Fic]—dc22
2003012503

QUM 10 9 8 7 6 5 4 3 2 1

To Ellery, my rose
Skeet, lover of thorns
&
Kate, thorns and roses

Acknowledgments

Thank you to Richard Brenner for offering and giving generous help. For gifting me untold hours and late nights reading my words—for pointing with precision whenever I didn't hit it smack-on. Thank you for your expertise, poetic ear, passion, humor, verve, generosity, and gemelli.

* * *

Thanks to Ellery, my rose, for "getting" that a novel is An Event, and celebrating, and for your patience while waiting for life to get back "to the way it usually is." Kate for friendship, fierceness, and brilliance. Skeet for reading aloud, stunning art, clarity, and kindness. Mum for rooting and all those stories when I was young. Neal for always checking in—whether you need to or not. Greg for singing messages and odd information. James, James because, because . . . Bettie and Margie for your Grams's spirits. BH for gallop and patching bee holes. Suki for care packages and order. Chris for knowing "the creature is alive." Darilyn and Myra, for magical antness. Susie for your vibrant yes. Debbie K for poetry. Kim for leaving dinners and tiptoeing away. Lesley for keeping macramé at bay. Trish for supper by the sea. Molly for singing to rivers. Jay for finding mangoes. Steve for swooping in. Linda for connecting. My writing groups—feisty, awake women, and you too, Bob. The Kiwi Maxwells for adding our leaves to the tree. Sarah for roses. The Mead School, which honors kids and mine in particular. Charlotte for trees. Barb for blips. Shelly for searching me out to ask if I'd written a novel. OOD for putting us in touch. And Dinah for your gentle perspicuity.

1

I'M AN ISLAND IN THE MIDDLE of the hall. Kids stream around me on either side. I don't remember getting here, and I don't have the energy to break through the flow and escape. I just stand in one spot being bumped and smacked by backpacks as kids rush around me.

I'm thinking about a small sketch of a wasp posing on the porch railing that I struggled with this morning. There's an image behind the sketch I can't get to, like a reflection of trees in a lake that blurs and vanishes as wind disturbs the surface. Michelangelo, the great Renaissance painter and sculptor, said he saw figures in the rough-hewn marble before he ever picked up a chisel. He said the form was already in the stone and he just carved until he set the figures free. My sketchbook is filling up with unformed drawings because I've lost the ability to see and set them free.

Lockers slam, kids keep bumping into me.

"You're in the middle of the hall, weirdo!" shouts an observant idiot. "Not at a bus stop!"

"Move, mannequin," says the school's fashion queen,

tossing her hair, annoyed at having to swerve in her dangerously high-heeled shoes.

Then Mike Harkers, a guy who I swear hears crowds cheering for him wherever he goes, looms in front of me and comes to a stop. For the past three years I've watched Mike embarrass ninth graders, cheat on tests, and make rude comments as girls walk by. Once, as he passed the gym, I heard him refer to Charlotte Mase's rather remarkable breasts as lip treats. I call *him* Primate. He's the star running back on the school's football team and the top pitcher on the baseball team. He has thick brown hair and stunning dimples when he smiles. He smiles a lot.

Mike feeds on being popular and having girls hang on him. I *don't* hang on him, so he considers me a challenge. It seems to bug him that I don't give a flying pigskin what he thinks of me. He's been asking me out since ninth grade. I've been saying no since ninth grade. You'd think he'd give up. Or I would.

"Hey, Earth to Taylor," he says, smirking at me.

Now that Primate has landed on my island, the flow of kids alters its course, the way a current swerves around a rock.

"Are you in the building or have you left for lunch?"

Apparently, Mike never had an idea worth pausing for. If I'm lucky, he'll get distracted by a pair of passing breasts and take off in hot pursuit.

"So?" he says, poking my shoulder. "Are you in there, or what?"

I hate being poked, especially by people I don't like. "Stop it," I snap. "Just because a person doesn't answer right away doesn't mean she's spacing out. Some people actually have activity brewing inside their heads. Occasionally they even stop to examine an idea—you know, it's called thinking."

"Hey!" he says, shielding his head like a boxer who's about to be hit. "You don't have to go off on me. I'm just trying to make conversation."

"And I'm just trying to ignore you, which is what I always do. Did you think today was going to be *special?*"

I get sarcastic around Mike. I can't stop myself. The way he takes up space bugs me. It's like he needs more room to walk and breathe than anyone else at school.

"So what time should I pick you up for the prom?" he continues, blind to the possibility that there might be a girl in this world who wouldn't want to go out with him.

"When you stop being such a primate."

I never feel right with Mike. If my grandmother—who has more smarts about life than any other person I know—were here, she'd say, "Trust your intuition!" She'd also tell me to be myself no matter where I am or who I'm with. But I can't do that with Mike. I guess that's why I'm sarcastic—to protect myself from whatever it is that radiates off him. Talking with Mike makes me want to shower. I hate the way he leans over me and how he looks at me.

I plunge through a cluster of kids and make it into the

art room. As I walk over to my table, I shake my shoulders and hair as though I'm coming in from a dust storm.

RJ, my art buddy, is already here. "Shake it, baby," he says.

"Mike Harkers," I explain. "He just cornered me in the hall, and I think I got some of him on me."

RJ laughs as he rips up black and gold paper for the collage he started yesterday.

I used to feel welcome and at ease in the art room. When I'm into a project, time melts into luxurious inhales and exhales. I usually vanish so far into the materials and my work that when the bell rings at the end of class, my body jumps as if it's been struck. I'm desperate to get that deep-in feeling back. But today, once again, I just shove shapes around for a montage that never comes together. I'm less creative than a six-year-old poking peas around a dinner plate.

I glance over at RJ, who is totally into something. Usually he and I are so absorbed in our work, we create a buzz. Today it's just him.

I'm so shut down that I clean up even before the bell rings, a first for me. As I throw out scraps from yet another one of my art wrecks, I spot a poster for the Salt Rock Art Competition, which is open only to high school juniors. I've worked toward this goal since fourth grade, but now that I have the opportunity, I don't have the vision. Just seeing the poster makes my stomach tight, so when no one's watching, I rip it off the bulletin board and throw it out. Until now, I've been an art oasis, creations constantly springing out of me. Now, when I need new work for Salt Rock, I'm desert dry.

When I go back out into the hall, Mike is there, apparently undaunted by my endless rejections.

"Well?" he says. "Do we have a date?"

I look at him like he's a piece of lint on a wet painting. He touches my mouth with his index finger and I jump.

"Calm down," he says. "You had a piece of hair on your lip."

I glare at him. "Don't touch me without asking. Actually, don't touch me *ever*."

He looks startled. "I'm sorry, I just—I . . ." he says, and then he blushes. A deep red blush.

Suddenly, instead of looking around Mike to find a space to escape into, I'm looking right at him. I've never seen Mike vulnerable before, and it startles me. "I've got to get to lunch," I say, in a softer voice. I meet his eyes instead of averting mine, and I feel a trace of a smile.

For once he doesn't have anything to say. He just looks embarrassed and nods. I walk away.

I spot Barry Dunn in a stream of kids heading in the opposite direction.

"Hey, T!" he says.

"Horses," I say, passing him on my way to the cafeteria.

We've said "Hey" and "Horses" since we were little kids falling off bikes and scraping our knees. Grams said it first. It began as a joke, now it's a habit. Thoughts of Grams click on like Christmas lights whenever one of her lines, like "Horses" or my favorite, "Sip the sweet juice out of each of your days," slips into my head.

When we were little, Barry was at the house all the time. I called him Bears, he called me T. High school whooshed us apart in a whirlpool of new friends and activities. Moving up to ninth grade, meeting kids I didn't know and who didn't know me, gave me a chance to be new. When I was with Bears, I reverted to my kid self—old jokes, teasing—and suddenly I wanted more, so I stepped away from his familiarity. Distancing myself from Bears felt like an upgrade into adolescence. I figured he would always be there, and I wanted to sample new people.

But now, seeing his smile go by, I realize I miss him and the cozy friendship we shared for so long. First Bears, then Grams, and now my creativity have all vanished. Life is turning into a river sweeping parts of me away.

When I reach the cafeteria, I see my friend Ebbie, dressed in her usual black T-shirt and jeans, her wild hair sticking up like a patch of brown grass that the mower missed. She motions for me to join her and takes a huge bite out of a Braeburn apple as I sit down.

"Are you OK?" she says, shoving half her sandwich toward me.

"I couldn't get it going in art, again," I answer, shrugging and taking the sandwich.

We sit watching everyone eat. The cafeteria is a circus

prison gone mad. All the acts start at once and no one is audience except the kids who sit on the edges, hoping not to be noticed or torn apart, or perhaps just wanting out. Wardens march the perimeter, trying to keep us on our benches. Lunches are props. Some fly. Some are smooshed, some traded, and others dropped in perfect shape into the trash.

"This place is starting to feel too small," I say as we gather our stuff.

"I know it," Ebbie says. "I'm glad I'm going up to Canada this summer."

I love the Pacific Northwest and especially Whidbey Island, where we live. I've always loved our town because I feel safe here. I can walk anywhere. But sometimes I want to get off "the rock," the way Ebbie is going to, and go somewhere a thousand miles new.

TINY STARS TWIRL FROM GOLD threads over my bed. They came with putty for sticking them to the wall, but Grams and I think stars should dangle. Our stars spin and dance whenever a current of air touches them. A moon mobile I made in ninth grade hangs from the ceiling by the window. I think of the night sky as a black canvas painted with light. Because the moon is ever changing, I'm drawn to see what she looks like every evening. When

I was little, I called her my moon mother. I whispered secrets to her and blew her kisses before I fell asleep. I watched her swell and crescent. On nights when her light vanished from the dark sky, I imagined that she rested on our roof and fell asleep right above my room. I still watch her pale face from my window.

A cotton quilt, made by Grams, covers me with lavender stars and a gold crescent. On nights when the moon's full, she spreads silver across my bed. I sleep beneath two layers of moon and stars.

One star in the real sky is my own. Grams named it after me on my first birthday. Taylor Rose in the night sky. Taylor Rose in a house on Ellery Lane. Me in my house, the stars in their sky, everything solidly in place.

One evening in July when I was five and the moon was full, I asked Grams what happened to my mom, and she told me. My mother was taken out by a drunk driver. In one wrong twist of a wheel she was gone, and I wasn't even finished nursing. That night, the night my mom never came home, Dad and I moved in with Grams. While Dad wept, I lay content and sleeping in my grandmother's arms, and I've been held by Grams ever since.

After she told me this story, we looked out the window at the moon for a long time. I cried in my sleep, feeling the kind of sadness that doesn't vanish with cookies or even in Grams's sweet arms.

I've felt lucky I had Grams as my stand-in mother, though. Grams has always been centered on who she is, which makes it easier for me to be grounded in who I am. The hair on her head is short and sticks straight up. Straight up, just like she likes to live. She smacks her bare feet on the earth each spring and digs her toes in just to remember what grass and dirt feel like. She smells flowers the way she tastes wine—slowly, savoring each scent. Grams smiles wide and laughter splashes out of her like summer rain. She roars when she's angry, sobs when she's sad, and doesn't let anyone treat her mean. She knows how to shout "Yes!" to life. I grew up with that *yes*. Grams gave giant gold stars of *yes* to who I was. I was a *yes* until one blue-sky afternoon a week after Valentine's Day.

I was standing on the back porch, bundled up in my favorite periwinkle sweater, sketching the silver maple in our backyard. I could feel the whole Michelangelo thing going on as the sketch emerged right out of the paper. I was smiling up at the tree, feeling ecstatic, when I heard Grams making strange noises. She's always doing weird things like dancing the tango with the broom or singing original songs to birds. This time it sounded like she was trying to sing opera. I slid my sketch onto the porch swing and ran in the door laughing.

Grams seemed to be lying in snow on the kitchen floor. A crumpled angel, dropped from the sky. White flour was scattered all around her, the blue bowl lay tipped on its side beside her.

"Help! Oh my God, help!" I couldn't stop screaming.

Bears raced into the kitchen from next door. By then I

was crumpled on the floor beside Grams, holding her head in my lap and sobbing. Bears went for the phone. I heard him say it was an emergency and then give our address.

The only other thing I remember is Grams in the ambulance. Right before the doors closed, I saw the bottoms of her shoes. Gray and worn. I heard the ambulance doors close, but I didn't hear the doors inside me slam shut. Not that day.

3

THE SKY'S SEA GREEN, THE CLOUDS periwinkle blue, rainbow-colored stars cartwheel around an indigo sun, and a silver crescent moon twirls through vermilion grass. My hair is turquoise, with plums hanging from the ends, and I'm sailing over the moon on a sapphire fish.

That was my self-portrait from fourth grade. Everyone else filled the whole page with their face, measuring the width of the eyes and the proper distance between nose and mouth, just as the art teacher had taught us.

My self-portrait sits in an ornate gold frame. A purple ribbon dangles from it with *1st Place* written on it in a child's script. Although my teacher hadn't been impressed, I awarded myself first prize. The painting with its purple ribbon hangs over our fireplace, where Grams put it seven years ago.

Grams has been displaying my art since I picked up my first crayon. By now it's all over the house—paintings and sketches in frames on the walls, jingly chimes and funky mobiles dangling above doorways and from the ceiling. She has always encouraged me to live wide. But Alessa Rose Wickham, my Grams, who used to live life big, is shrinking.

Whenever I needed arms because I was scared or sad, I ran to Grams. She was constantly there, and even though she couldn't always make things better, she was always a comfort. Now, instead of consoling me, she's terrifying me. Instead of being my cheering section, she's silent.

I love my dad, but he doesn't know me deep down. He hardly knows who I am, let alone how to celebrate me. He has no idea that I can't make decisions if I have too many choices. That I'm afraid the house will crack open from summer thunder. Or that seeing mothers hug their kids makes me cry inside. He doesn't talk about stuff I need to talk about—Grams, my mother.

Grams used to fill up this whole house. Without her, it's empty. Now it feels like the Faloons' when they're on vacation and I go over to feed their cats. Nothing is wrong, but the place feels lonely without the smell of cooking, without the kids running in and out. As if a house isn't real without its people. Our house feels like it's waiting for us to come home, even though we're still right here living in it.

When I visit Grams in the Golden Edges nursing home,

I look only at her hair, mostly flattened now from all the time she spends in bed. Or I stare at her hands, when they aren't fluttering but just resting in her lap. I examine the shape of her fingers. They're almost the same as before, though they're not as fluid when they move and they seem more wrinkled. Lately, the hardest place to look is Grams's eyes. I used to sink into them and feel at home. Now when she looks at me—and isn't really seeing me—I feel lost, like a little kid in a swirl of unfamiliar faces.

The last time I went to see her, we were sitting in the same room but nothing happened. We didn't talk, smile, or even touch. This time we have a tiny conversation.

"Hi, Grams," I say to her hair.

"Roses," she says, staring out the window.

Her words used to flow strong, currenting along like a rollicking river, her hands setting the pace, like a master conductor. Now her words trickle out like the last few drops seeping from the end of a forgotten hose. Grams used to draw me in with her warm arms; now they lie in her lap, as limp as a sweater on the back of a chair.

I used to feel so wide and possible around her. Like the feeling I get riding a Ferris wheel, when I'm swooping around in the air, seeing far beyond the fairgrounds, across the water to the mountains on the mainland. Life was such a fun ride. I wanted more of it and always more of Grams. Now I'm shoving her away as if she's of no use to me. Doing that makes me feel like an empty grocery bag, flattened and crammed into a dark cupboard. The worst of it is that Grams is the one in trouble, and yet I'm the one flattening and packing myself away. *My* body still works, *I* didn't have a stroke. But I haven't done any decent artwork, not even a simple sketch, since that day I found her crumpled on the kitchen floor. The great well where my spirit and energy were stored has dried up.

Seeing Grams in this sterile place, where everything looks the same and she just sits there staring, is a nightmare. I want to either wake up or walk away. Every time I visit, I have to force myself up the steps of the home and drag the front doors open. The reception desk looks far away, as if I'm seeing it from the wrong end of a telescope. I feel frail, almost like one of the wizened ladies in there who lean sideways in their chairs, as if they're being blown over by a strong wind.

At first I used to ask the smiley nurses, "When is Grams coming home?" Their smiles would slide off each time as they said, "Your grandmother won't be coming home." They said it softly, like air leaking out of a balloon. I don't ask anymore. I just walk to Grams's room. Not so much walk as slog. I *slog* to her room. My shoes slump down the long hallway.

"What are you doing, Grams?" I mumble.

She seems to be staring at a truly ugly macramé of an owl that's hanging on the wall. It's frayed, has worn wooden eyes, and is brown, her least favorite color. The real Grams would never put up with this. She'd pitch that butt-ugly weaving out the door. Then she'd stomp out after it and race far from this sterile, dead place. Real Grams would hate it here.

"Want me to pitch that?" I ask.

She keeps staring as if she has no ears.

"I can throw that wretched thing out," I say, louder this time.

"Is it real?" she says.

"The owl?"

"Owl. It's not real, is it?" she says, in a used-Kleenex kind of voice.

"No," I say. "It's not."

She turns and looks at me, but her eyes don't seem to see me. She appears to be looking past me, somewhere off over my shoulder. When I turn and look behind me, all I see is the blank cream wall of her room.

She can't remember things again today, like my name. "I'm Taylor Rose, your granddaughter," I say, over and over.

It breaks my heart. I don't know how to talk real to Grams when she doesn't know it's me talking. Her arms are still right here, soft and warm, but they can't hold me right anymore. And now I don't want them anywhere near me.

"Where's Jimmy?" she asks.

"We don't know any Jimmy," I say, still angry that she can't remember me.

"He said he'd meet me on the porch swing," she says, talking to me and ignoring me at the same time—like she's talking to someone else, even though I'm the only one in the room with her.

"Who?"

"He'll bring roses. He always brings roses."

"Grams!" I shout, willing her to come back into herself. "Are you OK?"

"Who are you?" she says, staring at the stupid owl.

"Taylor," I say again. "I'm Taylor Rose, your granddaughter."

"We should all get roses," she says.

The whole time I've been here, she's been eating a muffin, and her chin is a mess. She has been so aware all her life, and now she doesn't even know when she has crumbs on her face. I hand her the napkin that's sitting right in front of her on the tray.

"Thank you," she says, slowly unfolding the paper as if it contains a delicate gift. "Pretty wings!" She swoops the napkin skyward with two fingers, gently tossing it up, letting it go, and watching it drift down onto the floor. Part of me can see that it's pretty, but most of me wants to kick the wall. I leave without even saying goodbye.

I'm angry at Grams for something that isn't her fault. We're abandoning each other. Her boat has come unanchored and is drifting downstream, away from the shore. Only it isn't her choice. I'm on shore, running in the opposite direction. I have a choice. And I'm running away.

The whole way home I blurt out every swear word I've ever heard, cramming them together into one long necklace. I repeat this necklace over and over until it's a chant. I'm still chanting as I bang into the house, letting the screen door slam behind me. Dad is sitting at the kitchen table and looks over the top of his newspaper as if a cannonball has been shot into the room.

"Hi!" I say.

He blinks at me.

"I just saw Grams."

"I hope you weren't saying all that to Grams," he says, folding the paper as if he's going to keep talking.

"No," I say, surprised to find myself smiling at Dad's little joke.

Dad smiles back, and we're stuck grinning at each other.

"What did Mom think of Grams?" I blurt out, wanting to have some kind of conversation with him. This is a new Mom question. Dad doesn't answer Mom questions, but I keep trying.

He looks like he's forgotten something and is anxiously trying to recall it. *Talk to me,* I think. I want to hear words, stories. Something interesting. I want him to fill up this empty house with words, but he's always left that up to Grams and me.

I try again. "What was Mom like?"

I've asked this question twelve hundred times. Grams told me lots of stories about my mom, but I want to hear some from Dad.

"Hard to say," he sighs.

"Forget it." I scowl and start to stomp away.

Dad reaches out and touches my hand. "There's an envelope on your bed that I think you've been waiting for," he says. "And Barry called."

The envelope has got to be from Salt Rock.

A long cream-colored envelope sits tilted on my pillow. Even from across the room I can see that *Salt Rock* is written on the top left corner in sea green letters. The moment I spot it, my furniture vanishes, posters fade off the walls, and even my rug of roses shrinks and disappears. My entire décor consists of one envelope balanced on the edge of my pillow. Suddenly I don't really know whether I want to get in or not.

First step is to be selected by your art teacher. I was. Next, Mr. Lee sent in work of mine for their consideration. Now, either I'm invited to enter new work or I'm patted on the head and told they're not interested. Getting in is a promise of entrance into the best art schools and beyond that to wild dreams of galleries, openings, champagne, red dots, collectors. . . . That's the fantasy, anyway. Here it is, the year I finally might get to submit. And after filling trillions of art pads my whole life, I'm coming up blank.

I turn the envelope in my hand, not ready to see what's inside. Reading the letter will be like tossing a stone into water. There are going to be ripples. *No* will feel bad, *yes* may feel worse. I'm a Ping-Pong ball bouncing back and forth between *yes* and *no* paddles. Neither side's a win.

Grams and I used to put on my own practice Salt Rock show every summer. I'd choose my best work and place it around the living room; we'd invite friends in for a viewing and serve drinks and food. The guest book from all those years is in my bookcase. Seven years' worth of rehearsals, and now . . .

Ansel Adams, my stuffed panda, is sitting on my bed. I pick him up, and then I slowly pull the envelope open. The paper inside is sea green, too.

"I made it," I say to Ansel. *Thud.* My voice sounds like a bag of flour dropped on a countertop. Grams and I should be yelling and dancing so hard we shake the teacups in the cupboard. I sit motionless.

I'm looking through the wrong end of the telescope again, and I see my small self slumped on my bed. I'm a photo in an old album, and underneath me it says, *Taylor receives her invitation for Salt Rock.* The photograph should be of me leaping on my bed, waving the invitation with a look of wild joy. I should be racing across the lawn to Bears's house clutching the invitation and shouting like an insane girl. *Thud. Slump.* I look like a lady in a nursing home.

A movement outside the window catches my eye. A crow is trying to balance on top of the silver maple. Grams says everything on this whole earth is a sign. It's windy, so the crow has to struggle to sit on the branch.

The pine with the straight-out branches would be better, but this particular bird doesn't seem to think so. This big old crow does dance steps just to stay attached to the floppy top of the maple.

I automatically reach for my sketchpad. I position my pencil on a page. But I can't find the place where ideas flow out onto paper. I don't draw one feather or bird toe, not one maple leaf. I've never gone so long without a single sketch. It's like Grams and I both had a stroke. I crumple my invitation into the wastebasket and weep.

When I can see again, I wipe my eyes and pick up my stuffed doll with the purple dress filled with stars. Grams gave Mai Ling to me when I was barely higher than the piano bench. I mutter at her when I feel like talking out loud in my room. I hold her and whisper, "I got invited to Salt Rock. I wish . . ."

Grams used to say wishes are good things to make—whether whispered to stars, tossed with stones, or uttered to a doll. I have two wishes now, which are more important than any I've ever had: that Grams could come back, and that I could return to the place where art flows out of me. However, right now, even if I tossed three thousand stones with three thousand wishes in three thousand oceans, I wouldn't believe a single wish would come true. For the past few months I've wished myself dry. I've probably made those wishes ten million times. Every night, the same two wishes. Every day, the same nothing.

4

WHEN I'M INTO ANY KIND of art project, sparks shoot around under my skin. Sometimes when I'm excited about a new idea, I feel that if I glance up quickly, whatever I look at will burst into flames. I used to think my body was 76 percent ideas, not water. Whenever I had a blank page in front of me, I felt wings poised for landing. I never had to think what I might do. Ideas were air, always there.

I can still feel concepts hovering in my mind, but now I can't see them and they can't land. Back in ninth grade an author came to our school and spoke about writer's block. The whole time she talked, I sketched. I got pages of drawings done. I couldn't imagine not having ideas or not being able to express them. Now, without my fingers twitching to draw, I feel as flat as an airport runway.

"I have to do *something*. I've got to get *jazzed*," I say to Mai Ling. She's flopped over my knee, staring at the rug. I set her straight, pull my invite out of the trash, smooth it, give it to Mai Ling to hold, and go downstairs, to the cupboard where I keep my art supplies. I grab a handful of acrylic paint tubes, a few sticks of charcoal, a box of pastels, a few brushes, and a palette, and arrange them in a circle on the porch. I fill a small applesauce jar with water from the hose and place it in the circle. I set my easel in the middle, position a blank pad on it, and step away. Then I take three long breaths and step back into the circle.

"OK," I say. "I'm ready."

I stand still, waiting. I'm willing one skinny image to come skulking out of my brain to my fingers and onto the paper.

I pick up the brush, dip it in water, and tap it on the edge of the jar like an orchestra conductor tapping the baton. Next I squirt blobs of crimson lake and saffron yellow on my palette, scoop a dab of crimson onto my brush, and wait. I hold the brush half an inch above the paper, hovering in dead air, but I can't even get a squint of an idea. I'm as blank as the page. So I pull my hand way back and dive-bomb the paper, making thuds with my brush. I smear red around and around in circles. Then I streak saffron slashes through the heart of the paper. Slash. Slash. I keep slashing until I have a bloody mess. Halle, the little girl down the street, could stir water into a pile of dirt and create something more interesting than this, and she's only seven years old.

I throw my brush off the porch and kick the jar of water with the edge of my foot. The glass hits a porch rail and shatters, strewing shards across the floor. Another wreck by Taylor Rose Wickham in her ongoing series of worthless crap.

"This sucks!" I say dramatically, one hand pointing to the wreck on my easel and the other to the glass smashed on the floor. With my arms outstretched, I must look like

I'm ready to fly off the porch, but I can't get off the ground.

I grab the dustpan, sweep the pieces into it with the bottom of my sneaker, and head back up to my room. I fling Mai Ling off my pillow and watch her fly into the bookcase. She lands near the journal Grams gave me for Christmas, which I threw off my bed yesterday.

"Sorry, Mai Ling," I say, picking her up and straightening her dress. Then I open the journal. There's only one entry in it. I wrote it last week in the nursing home.

Sunday, April 27, 3 P.M.

> *Alessa Rose glances around this room she's in.*
> *Contained in a place unfamiliar and thin.*
> *It's like she just arrived on this old planet*
> *instead of having spent a whole life living on it.*
> *Her entire life's folded and packed away tight,*
> *everything familiar swept out of sight.*
> *She relished her days, wildly alive.*
> *Now she's wasting, waiting to die.*

I flick the journal's cover, remembering what Grams said when she gave it to me. "Your mind's a feast. Write those rich ideas of yours down."

"I don't write, I paint," I said back.

"You *think*," she said. "Artists write, too. You devoured the letters that Vincent van Gogh wrote to his brother Theo."

"Thanks, it's a beautiful journal," I said, still not convinced. Then I opened the cover and found that Grams had inscribed it with one of my favorite quotes from van Gogh's writings: "I am trying to get at something utterly heartbroken."

Despite Grams's suggestion, I was so lost in my painting that I never took the time to write, and the journal sat unopened in my bookcase until last Sunday. *If I can't draw anything anymore,* I said to myself, *I might as well try words.*

I get up to stretch and wander down the hall. As I pass Grams's room, I get a weird feeling that she's in there and poke my head in.

"Hi, sweetheart," says Dad, who's sitting in Grams's flowered chair.

"Oh!" I say, catching my breath and trying to breathe normally. "Hi."

"I didn't mean to startle you," he says quietly.

"Are you OK? What are you doing in here?"

"I don't know," he says. "I was just . . . I was . . ."

"Thinking about Grams?" I say.

"Yes."

I go in and click on the light. He's clutching a framed picture of my mom and Grams. He looks embarrassed. I feel embarrassed. I don't know what to say, and I wish I hadn't found him here.

"Chinese?" says Dad.

"Chinese?" I repeat, confused.

"How about takeout from Ming's Garden for dinner tonight?"

"Oh, yeah, great," I answer, with mock enthusiasm, as if this won't be our third straight dinner from Ming's. "Chinese is good."

I wish I'd lean in and look closely at the picture he's holding. Or squat down next to him and look at it with him. I wish I'd say something about Mom, about Grams. About anything. But I don't. I feel like a frozen snowgirl wandering around in a blizzard, peering in windows, wishing I felt human and warm and could sit cozy beside a fire and talk about all the things I need to talk about. But I'm stuck inside the freezer that's my heart. I'm so stiff and cold that all I can do is say "Chinese is good" and walk out of Grams's room.

"THIS PLACE STINKS," I think as I sit in Grams's room at the Golden Edges. It's a moldy mixture of a dentist's waiting room, stale breath, and the dissection table in our high school biology lab.

"Pay attention."

I jump and look up. Grams is staring at my journal. I wait. She doesn't say anything else.

Grams taught me how to pay attention, and she cheered when I played with my imagination. Paying attention is being aware of things as they are. Like the crow and the silver maple—not making them into anything but black bird and green tree. Noticing every detail and drawing them as they are. Imagining is fooling around with how things could be—tiny pirate commandeering leafy boat.

"We should all get roses," Grams says suddenly, and I'm jolted out of my head and back into her room. Even though she's freaking me out, I still think that's a sweet thing to say. I write down *Pay attention* and *We should all get roses*. Her eyes aren't in this room as she speaks, and I wonder if she's dancing somewhere with roses in her hands or sitting on a porch, sniffing a long-stemmed rose. Perhaps there's a secret password to the new place in Grams's mind—*roses* or thoughts of roses or the act of remembering roses.

"Roses," she says again as if uttering a spell that will make roses bloom, *poof,* right in her lap. She's even holding her hands curled and slightly open, as if she's ready to receive a bouquet.

"Sweet roses in the air," she whispers from wherever her mind is.

I miss hearing how Grams thinks, and I miss her attention. She had a talent for listening. She listened to me like a jazz aficionado, tapping along with the beat of my stories, relishing the twists and turns. Without Grams, I feel as though I've lost my chops, the lights are out, and the audience has all gone home.

My fingers start flipping the pages of my near-empty

journal back and forth. I twirl the pen around in my fingers, then place the point on a page and make one dot. I don't want to write how I feel because I might crack apart if I looked inside myself.

"Jimmy!" Grams says suddenly. "Where's the porch swing? Where's Jimmy?"

"I don't know a Jimmy, Grams. The porch swing is on the porch."

Grams looks at me as if I've dropped out of the ceiling tiles. "I want one of those square sweet things with the pink icing," she says.

"Cake?"

"I want cake!" she says. "Birthday cake."

"I could bake you one tonight, the kind we used to make together, and bring it here tomorrow."

"Why don't they put roses all over?" she asks me.

"I don't know," I say. "They should."

"We should all get roses," she says again. "Everyone should get roses."

"That's true, Grams. We shouldn't have to settle for parts of words and leftover leaves." I say all this calmly, but my stomach's writhing around like an earthworm on a sidewalk.

"I'll make cakes full of roses," she says. She nibbles at a muffin that has been sitting on a napkin in her lap.

"That would be good."

"Three," she says, slowly counting her fingers. "Three roses for every piece."

There's a mirror beside her chair. She turns, and her reflection catches her eye. She stares at herself and so do I. Her neck has turned into a limp skin curtain that hangs from the bottom of her face and disappears into the top of her sweater. I've never watched her so closely before.

"Old frog," she mutters, and frowns.

She pulls a hanky out of her sweater sleeve and dabs the corners of her mouth, but misses most of the crumbs. She kisses the hanky when it touches her lips. I'm sad to think that white cotton handkerchiefs may be the only things that kiss her lips anymore.

"Max . . . kisses!" she says, startling me with a similar thought. "I like kisses."

"Yeah?" Max is my dad, Max is her son.

"He kissed me a thousand times."

"Dad did?"

"Jimmy," she says.

Then she looks right at me. "'You're as sweet as raspberries. As perfect as a rose,' he said. He never came back."

Suddenly, Grams looks like she's melting. Her eyes and mouth crumple in on themselves, and she's crying. I tear out of the room and race down the hall yelling for a nurse. When I find one, I grab her and point toward Grams's room. "Down there—Grams's room—my grandmother—hurry!" I walk away quickly in the opposite direction, feeling like a traitor and a wimp.

As I shove open the doors to escape, Mindy, my former best friend, is just coming up the sidewalk. I want to leap into the bushes to avoid her, but we catch each other's eye, so I wave. Last year our friendship vanished as silently as childhood fades. We never had a fight or agreed not to be friends, we just slipped away from each other. It was like the very last time you play a childhood game. You don't know, racing around in the settlling autumn twilight, that this is the last time you'll ever play freeze tag. You wave goodbye to your friends and go in for supper, never suspecting that you've just closed a chapter in your life. As you're crunching carrot sticks, the season suddenly switches, and when spring comes around, you're playing other games. My friendship with Mindy was like that, a piece of life that slipped away when I wasn't paying attention.

"Hey," I say as we meet on the sidewalk.

"Hi," she says back, looking no happier about this chance meeting than I am. She flicks hair out of her face, but it falls right back and covers her left eye. She's wearing a loose shirt the color of tangerines and a belt woven with turquoise and gold threads.

"What's up?" I say.

"Going to visit my aunt Min. She's in there," Mindy says, nodding toward the Golden Edges.

"I didn't know. I'm sorry."

"Old Min was the only one who got me," she says.

I used to get Mindy, but she slowly morphed into cool and boy-crazy, and I was totally absorbed in art.

"I hate this place," I say. "I was just with Grams. She's in here now, too."

I'm looking at the face of a girl I watched grow up. I saw her first zit right there on her forehead. We compared our breasts as our right ones grew faster than our left. And now we're on a sidewalk, each in our own square.

"Oh," says Mindy. "Grams must hate it in there. How is she?"

"Not so great."

"I can't imagine Grams in a place like this." Mindy's saying the right things, but it feels as if she's standing on the mainland and talking through a mist.

"Grams is freaking me out. She usually doesn't remember me, and she says weird things."

"It's a really crappy thing to happen to her," says Mindy, fingering her belt. "I've got to go, Taylor. See you." And off she walks.

I feel as though she just hung up on me.

Before going back to my house, I walk over to Whitcomb Hill, the place that Grams and I thought of as our second home. I love wandering over the wavy meadow, watching bees dipping for nectar and tipping buttercups over onto their lemon-colored sides. On my way up the hill I pass through groups of bleating sheep. They skitter away when I get too close, their hooves striking rocks as they run. From the top of Whitcomb Hill their puffy bodies look like slowly moving clouds as they amble across the meadow, grazing on grass and flowers.

At the top of the hill is a huge rock that Grams and I named Victoria Rose: Victoria because she's strong and independent, like the nineteenth-century English queen; Rose because we wanted her to share our middle name. The rock became our sanctuary, the place we'd visit on Sundays instead of going to church. Sometimes it was our crying place, like when Bok Choy, our white-pawed, black-haired cat, disappeared. And on the day after Grams told me about my mother's death, we came up here to celebrate her life. We lit a candle, and Grams told her favorite stories about my mom. Then Grams read poems she knew my mom loved. I still have the list: Emily Dickinson's "I shall not live in vain," Billy Collins's "Aimless Love," and a poem by Mary Oliver called "The Summer Day."

I've left gifts on the small shelf near the top of Victoria Rose for as long as I can remember—seashells and sea glass, heart-shaped rocks, and once a four-leaf clover that I've sometimes wished I'd kept.

Victoria Rose glitters in the sun today. I rest my back in a smooth spot near her base, absorbing her warmth, and stretch my legs through the long grasses. Gazing down over my town, and out across Puget Sound, makes the tight places in me uncoil. I take in the beauty of the water and feel the silky air on my skin, the comfort of this spot, and the welcome relief of tears softly slipping down my cheeks.

When I get home, something feels strange. I stand in the kitchen, squinting, trying to figure out what it is. It feels as if the house has died, as if its heart has stopped beating. . . . The hall clock! It isn't ticking. I've forgotten to wind it. Grams used to wind this old steeple clock as faithfully as she made my school lunch every morning. I notice it only when it's silent.

I yank open the little door on the front, rummage for the key, and begin to wind. I'm thinking about an old song—a grandfather clock that stopped, never to go again, when the old man died—and I feel desperate to make it tick. Somewhere in my superstitious heart I'm afraid Grams might die if I forget to wind her clock.

It's ticking again, but I decide to call the Golden Edges anyway.

"Hi, this is Alessa Wickham's granddaughter speaking. Would you please go see if my grandmother's OK?"

The nurse tells me that Grams is fine, that she just served her a nice supper of chicken and rice.

"Please just check again."

There's a rustle. I hear the nurse's shoes ticking down the hall and then silence. Shoes, rustle, and Grams is still fine.

"Thank you," I say.

I grab a piece of paper and write: *WIND THE DAMN CLOCK!!!!!* I magnet it to the refrigerator before yanking the door open to inspect the contents. There's nothing tempting to eat. Nothing. I can't get used to the idea that unless I go out and grocery-shop, stuff is not going to show up. Grams is not down at the Star store gathering dinner supplies. She's not about to shoot through the door and make us something to eat. Dad's too busy on some work project to go shopping for food on a regular basis—he just picks up our dinner on the way home each night. And this damn refrigerator does not produce meals the way a chicken bloops out eggs.

"Hi!" says Dad, coming in the kitchen door.

"Hey," I say. "We don't have interesting food in the house."

"Oh?" he says. "What sort of interesting food? Blue milk? Cheese that sings?"

"Ha," I say. "Very funny."

Dad has never shown much interest in food. Grams loved it. She didn't like making it as much as she liked finding it. She named one of her African violets Vindaloo after a spicy Indian dish. Our fridge used to be packed with so many intriguing things, opening it was almost like traveling abroad.

"I just saw Mamma . . . Grams," Dad says.

"Me, too," I say. We are the supreme example of ships passing in the night. "Pissing in the night," Mindy and I used to say.

"I'd like to go together sometime. Would you?"

"I don't know," I say, feeling myself shut down. Everything interesting about me slams closed when Dad walks in. I am never how I want to be. There's no chance he'll ever get to know me because I don't show up when he's around. This boring girl shows up instead.

"Chinese?" says Dad, shifting into a conversation we can deal with.

"Sure," I say. "Chinese is good."

THE BELL RINGS. *Bam!* We slam our textbooks shut. The room shudders with the sound. We hustle to get out. Backpacks swing onto shoulders, kids call to friends. Out in the hall, locker doors crash. Shouts bounce off the walls. We scurry around the tunnels of school like ants.

Ebbie and I keep colliding as we navigate the chaos of the hall. Usually, we feel like cows being herded. Sometimes we say, *"Cows,"* stop dead, and moo. We're sworn at and bumped into, but it makes us laugh, so we do it anyway. We know it's childish, but we love it. Maybe that's *why* we love it.

Today I stop and say, *"Ants!"*

"What?"

"Ants," I say again, making antennae with two fingers and waving them around.

"I thought we were cows."

"After seeing that movie in class, I've changed my mind. We haul stuff around and scoot from chamber to chamber like mindless insects. We're ants."

Ebbie laughs and makes antennae, too.

"See you tomorrow, weirdo."

"Yup," I say, wiggling my fingers at her.

Something inside me shrinks when I walk into school. School feels too small for who we are. What if education wasn't about getting A's, but about being true to yourself? Acting cool would automatically give you an F. What if school was a place to discover how unique each of us is, or could be? A place to wear *your own* creations, say what *you* think, and find out what *you* love. Anyone copying others, repeating someone else's answers, or not knowing what she was passionate about, would fail. You'd pass only if you were excited and into your own life. Graduation day would be a celebration of our originality: our clothes ablaze with turquoise, plum, and magenta, scarlet, gold, and vermilion; hundreds of colors and designs; our hair sweeping off our heads in as many styles as there are graduates. The PA system blaring our original songs, poems, and outlandish opinions. Instead of yearbooks filled with projections of imagined futures, we'd present what we'd already created: our novels, poetry, paintings, symphonies, ragas and rap tunes, scientific discoveries, new math formulas, environmental strategies, and peaceful solutions for the planet.

Graduation wouldn't be merely switching a tassel from one side of a flat black hat to the other. Graduation would be a teeming ocean of creativity pouring out of the school and into the streets.

My locker has always been the one place at school that feels like it's mine. I start a new collage on the inside of my locker door every September and add to it right up till the last week of school in June. I paste up photos, notes from friends, sketches, earrings, pieces of colored paper, parts of paintings, and portions of posters. By June all the metal has vanished beneath a barrage of art.

In tenth grade Ebbie got the locker I'd collaged the year before. She says she knew she wanted to be friends with me on the first day of school when she swung open the door and saw *Taylor Wickham* signed in swirls of purple, gold, and green.

Mindy and I were too tight back then for me to take much notice of Ebbie when she first got my old locker and told me how much she loved it. But after Mindy and I drifted apart at the beginning of the school year, Ebbie's friendly laugh drew me in, and soon we were eating lunch together every day and liking how each other's mind worked.

Even though this year is almost over, my locker is only partially done. It's sad to swing open that door and see dull green metal where there should be streaks of color, pieces of paper curling and layered, dangling or sweeping across the door, glittering jewels, sequins, parts of poems. Only half of the metal has vanished. Just a beginning of what this year's locker might have become.

The week after I told Ebbie about Grams having a stroke, she gave me some little wind chimes: a purple cow with little aqua udders dangling below. I hooked the chimes to the inside of the vent on my locker door, so whenever I open the door, the udders jingle.

"Reporting for ant duty!" Ebbie mutters the next morning as I race up and swing my locker open, wildly jingling the udders.

"Got my crumbs," she says, holding up her lunch. "Get in line, follow the path." We step into the rush of kids and march off to class.

I raise my binder above my head. "Leaf-cutter ant?" she guesses. I nod. Ebbie's trying to cheer me up, but all I can muster in return is a nod and a grimace of a smile.

Ebbie reaches over and squeezes my arm. "How come you're late again?"

"My alarm doesn't live in my house anymore," I say.

Grams used to wake me up. Slow and sweet. A kiss on my cheek.

I slouch in French class and stare blankly out the window. *Mon dieu.* The huge and varied world outside our anthill doesn't seem to count in here. I can get information from books and life experience from life. So where does school fit in? The only parts I like are art; the in-betweens, like free period and lunch; and the final bell. The art room's a place where it's truly OK to be different. It feels alive, like my house did when Grams was around.

I think about my last visit with Grams. I ran away when she cried. She's been there for me my whole life, but now when she needs me, I take off and run away. On the top of my French notebook I scribble *Mauvaise. I am evil.* The bell rings and I follow the line out the door. *Au revoir, français.*

"Hey, Leader Ant," says Ebbie, meeting me on her way to one of the lesson chambers.

I nod but keep walking.

"Hey!" Ebbie scrambles across to my lane. "Are you OK?"

"I'm an asshole," I mumble.

"Ant hole?"

"No, I'm an *ass*hole," I say again, so loud this time that kids turn and stare.

Ebbie touches my arm. "What's wrong?"

"Me. I'm wrong. The woman who raised me and loved me is not being loved back by me. My grandmother raised an asshole," I say, my voice reverberating down the hallway.

"Miss Wickham," says The Voice—our vice-principal and chief disciplinarian, who was hired to bother as many students per day as he can.

"Hi, Mr. Debot," I say, smiling as though I might actually be happy to see him.

"That was unusual language for a school hall," he says, breathing over Ebbie's shoulder.

I want to say, "Don't punish Ebbie by breathing your reptile breath on her. She hasn't done anything wrong." But he's too lame to know he punishes kids just by exhaling in their direction.

"We were discussing the film on *ant* holes," says Ebbie, swooping in to the rescue.

Mr. Debot looks confused. He rocks back on his heels, and then he smiles. "Excellent for students to continue class discussions in the halls," he says. "Carry on."

"You're going to have to be a quieter asshole," says Ebbie after he leaves.

"OK," I say. "See you, ant hole."

After a boring history class on some boring war a billion years ago, I head to my locker to get my lunch and remember that I forgot to make it . . . again! What an ant hole! I rummage in the small zippered pouch in my backpack for money. Grams used to tuck a few dollars in there each week. I scrape around and find thirteen cents. Since Grams left, this is about the hundredth time I haven't had lunch. At least ants find crumbs. I know Ebbie will share, but I don't want her thinking she has to feed me all the time.

As I walk into the cafeteria, she waves me over and watches me sit down. I pour a pile of white salt onto the black cafeteria table, smooth it out, and begin to draw in the granules. The grit of the salt feels good as I slide my finger around the table, making spirals. When this is all I do, Ebbie opens her lunch bag and lays everything out like I used to do with my night's haul of trick-or-treat candy on Halloween. "Apple, I only want half; sandwich, peanut butter and jam, slightly squashed—sorry—half is yours; salt and vinegar chips; one warm soda; and five cookies—you can have them, I'm sick of Oreos," she says.

"Thanks," I say, starting in on a cookie.

"You're not an ant hole," she says. "You're way too big."

7

"HEY, TAYLOR!" says RJ.

I nod.

"See you in the art room for free period?"

I shrug. I just don't feel like talking anymore. I don't refuse. I don't make an announcement, and I'm not totally silent. Mostly, though, I just nod for yes and shake for no. Not talking feels similar to wearing headphones. No obligation to respond to the outside world. Just moving through air. I am Shrug. I neither care nor care that I don't care.

A snake's brain is like a one-note hum. Not much registers except the occasional mouse. *Hmm . . . blip* (mouse) *. . . hmm.* I feel emotionally flat, as though I've had a transplant and been given a snake's brain.

Ebbie notices right away that I grunt more than I talk. She starts meeting me after each class and walking me to the next one. I feel like an inmate or a mental patient.

"Taylor?"

Her voice makes a blip on my brain, and I turn my head toward her.

"Are you OK?"

I nod.

"I'm here if you want to talk."

I nod again. We keep walking into the cafeteria and sit down.

"Is this about Grams?"

I shrug.

"Your art?"

I shrug again and watch a fly land on the edge of the table. It cleans its feet like a cat.

"Hey," she says. "Talk, Leader Ant. What's up with you?"

I look at her then. I know she cares about me. Her eyes, so full of concern, could make me cry. I look away and start scrabbling through my backpack, pretending to search for something. Ebbie leans across the table and strokes my hair. It is such an intimate gesture, and her touch is so tender and sweet, it feels as though she wants to comb my tears and sadness out like tangles. I jump up and rush into the hallway before I start sobbing.

I slam through the first exit I come to, fleeing past the Dumpster and into the lair of the serious smokers. RJ is standing there, his back to the world. When the door bangs shut, he turns around, and I see that he has painted ART RULES in big red letters on the front of his black T-shirt.

"Hey, Taylor."

When I don't say anything he says, "Want a toke?" and holds out a joint.

I've never wanted to smoke *anything*, but I nod and nonchalantly reach for the reefer. I take my first-ever hit as RJ tells me to inhale the warm smoke that's in my mouth. But as I try to do it, my throat constricts, and I cough everything out that I'd sucked in.

When I'm finally breathing normally again, I hear someone call my name. I turn to see Ebbie and Bears striding toward me like a sheriff and her sidekick. They plant themselves in front of me, warily staring at the joint held between my thumb and index finger.

Swirls of smoke spiral upward, painting the air. The only sound I hear in the sudden silence is the chattering of a sparrow. I see Ebbie's hand slowly moving toward my hair. I duck, turn, and run.

Later Ebbie calls me at home.

"What's up with you?" she asks.

"I'm busy, Eb," I say dully. "Gotta go. Bye."

I'm still holding the phone when it rings again. I drop it on the kitchen table, backing away as if it might bite. It rings again as Dad's car pulls into the driveway, and keeps ringing and ringing, even as I'm swearing at it to shut up. Just as the car door slams, the phone finally goes silent, and I start to breathe again. In the silence I realize that the clock's not ticking.

As I'm scrabbling around to find the key to wind the clock, Dad walks in carrying an eggplant.

"Do you have any idea what to do with this?" he asks. "Constance left it on my desk with a note that just said, 'Enjoy!'"

"It's an eggplant, Dad," I say. "Like Grams used to use in that Greek moussaka dish."

"I love that dish," he says, looking at the dark purple shape as if it might magically poof into moussaka in his hands.

"Yeah, well, you have to cook it and mix it with stuff," I say, finding the key and giving the clock a good wind.

Heading back into the kitchen, I hear Dad's briefcase thud as he drops it beside the hall bench. When he comes in, I'm staring at the Chagall calendar that Grams hung on the kitchen pantry door. This month's picture is of a woman in a black dress with lace trim, holding a bouquet of roses. A man in a green shirt is flying above her and has turned his head to kiss her. The carpet below them is red, and they're moving toward an open window.

"Have you eaten yet?" Dad asks.

I nod absently as I fly over the red carpet, heading for that window.

Each step up the stairs to my room feels like three steps down inside my gut. My own father doesn't even notice that I no longer have anything to say. Nothing new, I guess. But with Grams gone, I notice his absence more. What *is* wrong with him? Why doesn't he talk to me like a normal person would? Do I have a broken dad, or is it me?

By the time I reach my room I'm angry and crying. Living with Dad isn't like living with a live human being. He's almost as silent and still as Mai Ling. Saying "Have you eaten yet?" is not enough. I need a real father who talks, not a damn stick figure who just nods when we pass in the hall. But this is exactly what I have with my father, a nodding acquaintance.

I kick open the door to my room, sending it banging against the rubber doorstop. I hear the phone ring downstairs and then Dad's voice. "Taylor, it's for you."

I slide the window open and slip out onto the roof. I'm halfway to a large overhanging limb of the silver maple when I see Bears leaning on his bedroom windowsill, a phone in his hand, waving at me. I wave back, and he points to the phone.

"Taylor?" says Dad from inside my room. He leans out the window with the cordless phone. "It's for you. It's—"

"Bears," I say impatiently, taking the phone from his outstretched hand. "Thanks."

"Hi," says Bears.

I wave.

"What's up?" he asks.

I shrug.

"Lose your voice?"

I sit cross-legged facing Bears and breathe into the phone.

"Are you sick?"

This time I shake my head no, for variety.

"Meet me at the gate," he says, and hangs up. We used to meet at the garden gate between our houses all the time when we were kids.

I drop my hand limply to my side, still holding the phone, and sit staring at his empty window. The phone rings again. I recoil and pitch it into the air. I watch it ring into the sky and then all the way down to the ground. When it smacks the grass, it stops ringing.

I climb back in my window, clomp down the stairs, and find Bears.

"What's up with you, little girl?" he asks, leaning on the gate. "Since when did you become a doper?"

I kick the dirt in the garden by the fence.

"You smoke joints. You shrug. You vandalize telephones. I know Grams taught us to live exciting lives, but I think you're missing her point," he says, smiling at me.

I crinkle my face in response and shrug again. I don't know what's going on with me, either. I feel stupid, and I don't even care about feeling stupid. Bears glances at the hole I'm making in the ground, and I notice the line he gets between his eyebrows when he's fishing for what to say.

"I haven't seen you at your easel in a long time," he says finally.

"I haven't seen you tie your shoes in a while," I say back.

"Have you decided what to submit for Salt Rock?" he asks, ignoring my snit.

I stop kicking dirt.

"Just 'cause we haven't been hanging out doesn't mean I've forgotten your big dream."

Silence.

"Taylor?"

I turn and stomp back toward the house. There's a purple blob on the porch; I must've stepped on a tube of paint on my way out the door. I stride into the ooze in my bare feet and watch my toes turn to plum. I tramp off the porch, plum footprints marking my way down the steps and along the path. The footprints fade as I walk farther. There's only a hint of a purple hue by the time I reach the rosebushes out front. I pad back to the porch and grab a tube of mint green. I squeeze a new blob halfway down the garden walk and watch my toes turn green. I'm off again, mint prints passing the plum's progress by fifteen steps. I do this again and again until a rainbow of missing persons have left our backyard and vanished at various places along the sidewalk.

THE NEXT DAY IN SCHOOL Ebbie comes straight to my locker.

"Talk!" she says.

I shove my books inside, jangling the udders.

"Well?" she says.

I shake my head no.

"So you're never going to speak again?" she says. "Great plan."

Ebbie shifts her books on her hip and rakes her fingers through her hair, making it stand up wild. She has about five hundred freckles on her nose, and I start counting them.

"Hello? Give me something here."

"Not now, Eb," I say, touching her arm.

As I turn away, she reaches out and pushes down a label that's sticking out the back of my T-shirt. Her fingers feel soft and warm on my neck as she pokes it back in.

"Nice prom picture," she says.

"What?"

She turns me around and points to the wall above my locker. Someone has taped up a poster that says PARIS IN THE GYM. There's a really bad drawing of the Eiffel Tower with our school's banner flying off the top of it and hearts flying around in the clouds.

"Ew!"

"Paris in the Gym. Poetic," says Ebbie, smiling at me. Then her face shifts. "Mike approaching to your rear," she whispers.

"I bought tickets to the prom," says Mike, looming over both of us. "I'm all set to take you to Paris."

"Fantastic," says Ebbie. "I love baguettes, and they have the best cheeses over there."

Mike suddenly looks uncomfortable. He must think

that Ebbie thought he meant *her*. Now he's unsure how to get out of it without embarrassing both of them.

"I'm just kidding, Mike," says Ebbie, taking pity on him.

"Oh, right," he says. "Well, I wouldn't have minded. So," he says, turning to me, "the prom? Will you go with me?"

I'm not going to get rid of this guy. And I'm not about to stand here arguing or throwing quips back and forth. "Whatever," I say.

"I'll take that as a yes," he says, and walks away.

Talking may be dangerous. But not talking *sucks*. At any other time in my life I'd have told him, "When you grow breasts!" Instead, I mutter "Whatever" and don't even set him straight.

"Earth to Taylor," says Ebbie.

"I can't believe that just happened."

"So either tell him you lost your mind and it's *n-o*, or think of it as a teenage dress-up experience. One night in your life as a generic teenager, like an experiment. Wear a low frontal garment," she adds before I can respond. "Render him speechless."

Ebbie spends our free period drawing disgusting prom corsages, boutonnieres, and footwear.

"Here's my best design so far," she says, sliding one over. "A large metal corsage shaped like the Eiffel Tower, worn between the breasts."

"That's a large bouquet," I say.

"If typical-male-teen-idol Mike tries to get too close, he'll be pierced or at least blocked by the corsage, leaving you free to do other things, like pick your nose." I know she's trying to get me to smile, but I feel like I have a cardboard face.

The next day in free period, Ebbie designs a boutonniere made entirely out of frogs' legs, plus open-toed shoes like the sightseeing boats on the Seine River in Paris. She draws faces on the toes like reclining sightseers looking up at Notre Dame Cathedral. Then she creates a pair of earrings that look like baguettes, those long, skinny loaves of French bread.

"My favorite is the frog-leg boutonniere," I say.

"Glue a bunch of legs together, attach a safety pin, and stick them right onto Mike's lapel," Ebbie says. "Very chic. I can get you a bag of those things—frogs' legs, not safety pins," she adds. "My uncle Jacques sells them in his market. But don't cook the little legs first. Leave them raw."

I raise my eyebrows at her.

"For the fresh scent," says Ebbie.

I nod and fill in the little feet on her design with a frog-colored pencil.

"What color's your dress?" says Mike, suddenly beside me. I jump, shooting a line of green across the frogs' legs, and quickly flip the boutonniere design face-down.

"What was that?" he says.

I give him a bland look.

"Can I see it?"

I shake my head.

"The little stained-glass window you did that's in the art room is cool," he says.

I shrug. I had no idea he'd ever been in the art room.

He's still staring at me, waiting for my answer, and a blush is spreading from his neck up to his forehead. It's the second time I've seen him do this. I feel an infinitesimal twinge about the boutonniere.

"Your dress," he says.

I blink, not sure what to say.

"What color is it? So I can get flowers to match."

Mike is twisting his baseball cap around in his hands like he's trying to wring it dry. I raise my eyebrows. He notices what he's doing and stops fidgeting.

"The cheerleaders have been talking about their dresses since January. I figured you'd have yours by now," he says.

I shake my head.

I want to shoo him off like a stray dog—wave my hand and say, "Go on! Beat it!" But I don't. That's probably the first time I've stopped myself from verbally biting him, but seeing him act halfway human is making it hard for me to brush him off. He doesn't know what to do. Neither do I.

OK, so what color is my dress most likely going to be? I should say "green" so my corsage can match his boutonniere.

I shrug.

Mike nods, realizing that his question doesn't have an answer. "OK. See you," he says, and walks off toward the gym.

"Have you lost your mind?" Ebbie says.

I nod. "I guess I'm really going to the prom," I say.

"I guess you really are. He's not as bad as he used to be. I saw him walk by a group of ninth graders the other day without devastating a single kid."

"Yeah, well," I say, turning the boutonniere drawing over and shoving it into my binder.

"See you, Prom Girl," says Ebbie. "I hear Paris is beautiful in the spring."

When I walk into the music room two periods later, Bears nods at me. There's an empty seat next to him and I slide into it. Even though we haven't been close since the beginning of ninth grade, I like when we're in a class together. It feels good to know Bears is there.

When the bell rings at the end of class, I realize that I've been sketching frog legs all over my notebook.

As he's scooping up his books, Bears leans over and says, "Mike? Did you actually say you'd go to the prom with *Mike?*"

I nod, feeling ridiculous and shy and stupid. Bears knows how much I've always detested Mike. Everyone does, really. It's kind of a joke in our school, how Mike asks me out and I refuse.

"Is that a yes?"

I nod and look around like I'm bored.

"You've got to be kidding! You hate that guy. What did he do, wear you down with his fake smile and dimples?"

"You sound like a jealous boyfriend," I say, feeling testy. I clutch my books and start out the door.

"What's up with you?" asks Bears, his voice so loud that other kids around us turn and look. "Talk to me, Taylor!"

I keep walking.

Bears gets in front and faces me. "Are you mad at me? Are you not talking to me or just not talking in general? What's going on?"

I shrug again. I'm trying to think of a response, but I'm snake brains again, and all I can think of to say is "mouse," which would make sense only to another snake.

Bears shakes his head and says, "Jeez!" He gives me a puzzled look and walks off. What am I doing? Not talking is starting to feel just plain stupid.

Just then Rod Blitt bumps into me, and I drop all the music sheets I was taking to my locker.

"Idiot," I say.

I don't know if I mean Rod or me.

I decide that my mute phase has gone on longer than even I can stand it. My first foray back into the land of conversation is with Ebbie.

"Should I get a dress that shows my crotch?" I ask her with a grin.

Ebbie drops her books on the floor. "Your *crotch?*" she shouts.

The entire baseball team is shuffling past, and Mike, who's with them, hears her. My face flame-broils.

"My *cleavage,*" I whisper, embarrassed.

When I was little, I thought *crotch* and *cleavage* meant the same thing. I once told a sales clerk I wanted a dress that showed my crotch, thinking I sounded grown-up. Grams hooted so loud that customers came around the dress racks to see what was going on. From then on we used to mix those two words up on purpose, but I didn't mean to do it today.

"You break your vow of silence with *crotch?*" says Ebbie.

"I didn't take a vow of silence," I say.

Ebbie raises her eyebrows at me. "You haven't said more than seventeen words since the Ant Hole Incident."

"I've been practicing self-restraint," I say.

"Well, it's good to have you back, Crotch Girl."

When I visit Grams, I tell her I'm going to the prom. "I told Ebbie I'm going to buy a dress that shows my crotch," I say. But she doesn't respond.

I let my eyes wander around her room. The way her bed is made, so stiff and perfect, it looks like dollhouse furniture, as if the covers are painted on. I shove my hands into my pockets and feel the money Dad left on the kitchen counter for a new dress. I say goodbye to Grams's body and set out to choose one.

Although I'm about to buy my first fancy dress for my first prom, I don't turn it into an event. I go into Second Time Round, a store that has hundreds of hand-me-down dresses, and buy the first fancy one that fits. It's mint-colored. Perfect. It will match Mike's boutonniere.

On my way out of the store I see Mindy.

"Hey," I say.

"Hi," she says. "What are you doing?"

"Shopping."

"Is it really true that you're going to the prom with Mike?"

I shift from foot to foot, feeling ridiculous, and say, "Yes, who'd have thought?"

When Mindy started going boy-crazy, Mike was all she talked about. I hated him and told her what a jerk I thought he was for months on end, so we argued all the time.

"You and Primate? I mean, I couldn't even believe it when I first heard—"

"I know," I say, interrupting her. "Neither could I."

"Well, take care of yourself, Taylor."

"What do you mean?"

"Well, Mike, he's . . . you know. I mean, he's not your type, is he?" she says. "Plus, you've always hated him."

"I don't know," I say. "It's just the prom. He's just a guy."

Mindy gives me a quizzical look.

"It's not a big deal," I say. "It's not an expedition into a volcano, it's just a dance."

"Listen," she says, but that's when Beth Lindgrin walks up.

"Let's go," whines Beth.

"Just a minute," says Mindy.

Beth pulls on her arm. "Come *on,* Mindy!"

"OK. Well, see you, Taylor," says Mindy. "Take care."

"Yeah. See you."

I watch Mindy, my old friend whom I don't understand anymore, walk away with Beth, a girl I never did understand.

9

PROM NIGHT, AND I FEEL as if I'm going to the dentist. When I yank my dress on and stare at myself in the mirror, I realize there's a lot of skin between my neck and the neckline. I race downstairs to the coat rack and grab a scarf that will cover me and not clash too badly with the dress. Before I can arrange the scarf, Mike raps a beat with his knuckles on the front screen door. He grins at the expanse of visible skin, glances at my face, then quickly dips his eyes and says hello to my breasts.

Seeing him stare at my breasts instead of looking me in the eye pisses me off, so I fling the screen door open and shove him. Hard. I catch him off guard and off balance, and he falls off the front steps and into the rosebushes.

"What the . . . ?" he says, looking up at me like I've grown scales and fangs.

"Oops," I say. As I lean down to help him up, I see him focus on my breasts again. The sight of my cleavage lulls him into forgetting I'm dangerous and he calms right down. Hypnotized.

"What was that about?" he says.

"Just a minute," I say, positioning the scarf securely over my cleavage. I saunter into the kitchen, where the frog's leg boutonniere is squatting in a plastic bag on the counter. I had taken pity on Mike this morning, bought a carnation, and made a lovely boutonniere for his lapel. But his inability to talk to my face, instead of my breasts, has caused me to revert to plan A.

I pitch the carnation into the sink, shove the truly disgusting boutonniere into my purse, and walk back to the front door.

"Ready?" he says.

"Oh, yes," I say, grinning at him like never before.

I like going into school at night. It seems slightly mysterious, almost as if interesting things could actually happen in this dull building. I forget that the lockers contain moldy sneakers and outmoded textbooks and that all the classrooms are painted puke green.

The gym's vanished, replaced with Disneyland Paris. There's an enormous papier-mâché replica of the Eiffel Tower with French words written in fancy script around the base. Most bizarre of all, the prom committee has created a fake waterway down the center of the basketball court. A painted wooden sign indicates that it's supposed to be the river Seine, which flows through the heart of Paris. There's a mural of a boat with people, who look like kids from the prom committee, waving a banner that says *Vive La France.* This attempt to cover the ugly wooden bleachers might have worked if we were all only three feet high.

After Mike and I have wandered around staring at papier-mâché Paris, I turn to him and announce, "And now for the finishing touch. The *pièce de résistance.* Close your eyes, *s'il vous plaît.*"

He closes his eyes and stands perfectly still while I drag the warm, limp, utterly disgusting boutonniere out of the little plastic bag and pin the stinky raw legs onto his jacket. *"Voilà!"*

"Judas Priest," squawks Mike before my hands get to my sides. "Tell me that smell has nothing to do with you."

"It doesn't," I say. "It's *you!*"

Mike is used to being popular and idolized. I doubt he's been shoved off a porch or pinned with dead frog parts before. Once he realizes the stench is coming from his lapel, he tears my smelly little surprise off and whips it away from him. I watch the little legs skid across the gym floor and vanish under the punch table. Mike wipes his hands on his pants legs about a hundred times and stares at me like I've turned chartreuse and sprouted fur.

"OK, so you really didn't want to come to the prom with me," he says.

"I really didn't," I say, feeling extremely uncomfortable but honest.

"But here we are," says Mike. "Do you want to dance?"

"Are you kidding?" I'd never want to dance with me after this.

"You at least owe me a dance."

And so we dance. We don't look at each other, talk, or even touch. We just dance, like we're each alone in our own private gym.

I run into Bears at the punch bowl while Mike's off relieving himself. Bears looks great. He isn't wearing a tux, like most of the guys, but slacks and a linen shirt with the sleeves rolled up.

"Aren't you the fashion rebel," I tease him.

"Suits are hell," says Bears.

"Poor baby."

"Having a good time with Mike?" he says, smirking at me.

I scrunch my face. "Yeah. A total blast!"

Bears smiles. "Nice scarf! Did you hand-paint it?"

"I did," I say, glad to have someone notice.

Bears takes a closer look at my scarf. "Beautiful. Had any punch yet?"

"Nope," I say, picking up the punch ladle and a cup.

"Don't," he says, taking the cup from me and pointing into the bowl.

I lean over and see that all the ice cubes have flies and bugs in them, and they're starting to melt, so little insect legs and body parts are floating around in the juice. "That's creative. Thanks for the warning."

"Anytime," says Bears.

"I brought something that would go well with this," I say, pointing to a fly's abdomen that's bobbing past my side of the bowl.

"Really?" he says, looking interested.

"Little froggies' legs, my contribution to the prom theme. I used them for Mike's boutonniere, but he decided against wearing them. They're under this table, if you want to add them in."

Bears lifts up a corner of the white tablecloth and peers underneath. "You have *got* to be kidding," he says, holding his nose. "What'd you do, say yes so you could mess with him?"

"No, I said yes because I'm stupid. This is how I redeem myself."

"I see," says Bears, straightening up. Mike walks up and grabs the ladle I've just put back on the punch table. "See you around the neighborhood," says Bears. "Great punch," he says to Mike, winking at me.

I smile.

I watch Bears saunter over to a girl in a shimmery blue dress. I've never seen her before. Her dress is perfect and her hair is perfect and her shoes match her dress. Perfectly. Then I turn and watch Mike drink three cups of punch. This is strangely satisfying.

When he finishes, he says, "Want some?"

"No thanks," I say. "You have bugs in your teeth."

"Right," he says.

"No, really."

"Right," he says again.

The next time I see Mike after the prom, he's coming my direction from way down the hall, but before we meet, he ducks into the nearest classroom. Now *he's* avoiding *me*.

Ebbie has a new name for me: "Her Greatness." I don't feel all that triumphant. Seeing Mike reminds me that he isn't the only jerk on the planet.

10

IN SOME FAMILIES, flipping the page over to a new month on a calendar may be no more eventful than replacing a roll of toilet paper. But at our house, the first day of every month was a big old celebration. It started the night before, when Grams lit candles and we said goodbye to the month that was ending. We'd name a few things we felt good about that had happened that month—the stunning leaves of the silver maple in October, finding the first crocus in March. The next morning she'd call up the stairs to me, "A new painting awaits unveiling!" This meant it was time to flip the old calendar page and reveal the next Chagall fantasy. Grams always chose calendars with reproductions of the work of the Russian painter Marc Chagall, who created scenes more vibrant and stunning than my wildest dreams.

Grams would wait for me to come down, and the moment I arrived she'd sweep the old month over with a flourish. "Ta-DAH!" she'd sing as the new picture was revealed, and we'd stand back to admire it. Grams would applaud. I felt sure Chagall would love Grams because his paintings seemed to revel in life the way she did.

Grams made Chagall seem like a close friend of the family. I believed this world-famous painter had created a calendar just for us. I used to wish he and Grams would get married. I told my second-grade teacher, Ms. Swann, that Marc Chagall was Grams's boyfriend. The morning after parents' night at my school, Grams cleared that up for me, explaining that the painter had died a long time ago.

When I was thirteen, Grams gave me a copy of an art book, *Chagall by Chagall.* Between the covers I discovered horses carrying bouquets and a woman off into a red sky; a red and yellow circus performer dancing naked on a yellow horse beside a blue-green cello player; sunset roses spilling from a blue-gray-rose woman holding an indigo fan and floating above them, while colored dreams soared above somber villages into the starry night.

Last year, when Grams announced she was taking me to Europe to see some of Chagall's art, I was thrilled. As the plane landed, I felt like we were swooping down into a fairy tale, and that feeling of enchantment stayed with me for the whole trip. The last stop on our tour was Zurich, where we found a cozy room in an inn on a cobblestone street. Our room had a view of the slender spire of a cathedral that houses stained-glass windows painted by Chagall.

Usually Grams had more energy than I did, but looking back, I realize she was starting to slow down even then. She rested a lot between excursions and took an afternoon nap nearly every day. After we'd unpacked, Grams was feeling too tired to explore, but I couldn't wait, so I asked if I could check out the cathedral on my own.

I love churches between services, when they're empty. Some are melancholy quiet; others are the kind of quiet I experience at night when it's snowing, and it feels as though the snow is wrapping me in dreams. In silent sanctuaries, I feel wide, still places inside myself that I don't feel anywhere else.

But there was so much energy shooting off the windows in this cathedral, I didn't think about snow or silence. I could not believe how totally cool those stained-glass windows were. Vibrant, crazy, wild images on church windows, where I thought art was supposed to be somber!

"*Whoa!*" I said, right out loud.

"Incredible, eh?" said another voice.

Startled, I whipped around to see a guy about my age with a drop-dead handsome face.

"Amazing, eh?" he said, with a British-sounding accent.

"I *know* it," I said. "Seeing Chagall's work makes my fingers twitch."

"*Exactly,*" he said. "Do you paint?"

"Yes," I said.

He had on jeans that were ripped at the knees, just like mine. He rested his left foot on one of the steps in front of the altar, and forest green and cerulean blue paint showed through the rip. There was a splotch of topaz on the edge of his T-shirt pocket and a dash of garnet red on his cheek.

I pointed to the paint on his knee. "You, too?"

He smiled and held out his hand. Canary yellow on his knuckles, a spot of plum on his middle finger . . . and the most adorable dimples in his cheeks.

"James," he said as we shook hands.

"Taylor."

James Taylor. We both laughed.

"Are you from England?" I asked.

"Canada."

"Cool! They like you Canadians better than us Americans over here."

"I know," he said, smiling, and turned so I could see a red maple leaf on his backpack. "I make sure my Canadian flag shows."

"Don't want to be mistaken for one of us loud Americans, *eh?*" I said.

"You seem OK," he said, winking at me. "Are you here to paint?"

"I wish," I answered. "But I didn't think of bringing supplies with me."

"Well, if you'd like, you're welcome to use whatever I have." He swung his satchel off his back and opened it up so I could scan its contents. I chose a sable brush. We shared his palette and worked side by side on the floor, painting watercolor sketches of Chagall's windows.

After an hour or so, he leaned over and said, "You have something on your face!" He smeared my cheek with Prussian blue. I brushed a streak of crimson down his nose. And we were off: emerald on my shoes, indigo on his chin. A glob of saffron flew from my brush, missed its mark, and landed on a priest who had suddenly appeared.

"It's OK, he's Canadian," I blurted out, pointing at James's backpack.

We started laughing so hard that we couldn't even stop to apologize.

"Let's meet here again tomorrow," said James, after we'd finally settled down.

The priest shook his head, indicating that he didn't think that was a very good idea. But after we'd promised to keep the paint on the paper, he relented. Or is it repented?

James and I met at the cathedral the following two afternoons, taking breaks from painting to lean against each other and talk. On the third day we held hands. I called him Marc, he called me Chagall. At the end of the last day I gave him the painting I'd been working on. He gave me his. Coming home, I was so sleepy I forgot his painting in the airport.

That's something else I've lost that I think about a lot.

11

WHEN I WAKE UP ON SUNDAY morning, I've forgotten Grams is sick. "Grams!" I yell. "Grams! I'm going to . . ." Then I remember. Thanks mostly to Grams, I've spent my whole life sipping sweet juice out of my days and then—smack! Sweet turned bitter.

I slump downstairs to eat breakfast and find a note from Dad on the table: *Morning. Gone to the market to buy orange juice. Dad.*

I swing open a kitchen cupboard and two moths fly out. Gross. I open a cereal box. A moth flies out of it, too. "Gross!" I shout.

I try another box. Empty. I can't believe I put an empty box back in the cupboard.

While I'm rummaging around in the pantry, I notice Grams's Chagall calendar and realize that today is June 1. When I flip the page, there's a red person with an ass's head playing a blue fiddle. A woman is trying to hand the creature flowers, but her arm can't reach that far.

June 25 is already circled and starred. Streaks of purple, rose, and gold shoot from the numbers like fireworks. Grams has written *SALT ROCK!!!* and surrounded the words with gold stars and spiraling purple lines. My stomach clenches as I look at Grams's writing and imagine a day earlier this year when she was fine. I can see her flipping ahead to June, certain that I'd be accepted, that we'd celebrate together. I want to rip the month out of the year. A hole for June to match the hole in me.

I slap the screen door open and walk out to the porch. My paints are strewn all over the floor. I gather them into a pile on the top step and sit beside them. It's a stunning summer day, with light filtering through the maple leaves and dappling the lawn. I stretch and breathe it all in, then decide to get off my butt.

I go over to my easel. The fresh pad of paper I'd clipped onto it is now rippled, warped from moisture. Damn. I carry the pad back over to the top step of the porch and flip it open. I squirt Mars black onto my fingers and smash them into the paper, swirling my hand across the page. The paint feels cool, oozing up between my fingers. I'm in kindergarten again. Holding a tube of silver high above the pad, I squeeze, and a river of silver ribbons down. Then turquoise, crimson, purple, until there's a multicolored puddle on the page.

I mush my fingers into the colors, spiraling both hands

around and around till the paper rips and all the colors turn to mud. "Damn!"

I rip off that sheet and start another. I cover my fingers with midnight black, smack the page, and shoot dark sprays of midnight across the white paper. I slap down terra cotta and smear it everywhere.

"Taylor!" I shout. "What are you *doing?*"

I say this repeatedly as I grab colors, swipe them, smear them, all over the paper. Page after page. I'm breathing hard like I'm running. My fingers are the bristles and my arm the brush. I keep attacking fresh sheets until they tear and then I start again. I go through the entire pad without creating a single recognizable image. I haven't made this much mud since Bears and I made pies in his yard when we were four.

The next day in art class I have no idea what to do. I tell Mr. Lee, my art teacher, about my muddy messes.

"You're welcome to keep working on your new technique here," he says with a slight smile.

"It's not a *technique*," I shoot back. "It's *sludge*."

"That's OK," he says. "Creativity often emerges out of chaos. It's all part of the process."

I sling my backpack over the chair next to RJ's and grab tubes of acrylic paint from the drawer, choosing colors with names I like: Mars black, dark umber, titanium white, indigo, copper, silver. I squirt black onto my fingers and start another art attack. By the time I'm finished, my "work" looks like huge pieces of paper towel that have been used to wipe up paint in a kindergarten art class.

I do this every day for a week. RJ occasionally leans over to check my progress but doesn't say anything about the endless pile of thick smeary blobs, and Mr. Lee never mentions that I'm wasting paint, paper, and time. He treats me as if what I'm doing is a painful but necessary step in my development as an artist, which makes me feel a little less like a crazed idiot and more like someone trying to find her way.

Sometimes when I look up, I catch RJ's eye. He smiles or nods. "Ragin' finger paintin'," he says once.

I work in a frenzy, smacking the page, fighting to clear the muck in my brains.

As I'm ripping off another sheet and starting in on another round of paint war, a voice shouts, "Look out!"

Mike. It's the first time we've been face to face since I left him with bugs in his teeth. I shove past him to get more paint.

"I thought we finished finger-painting in kindergarten," he says with a fake laugh.

He's a house fly. Ignore him, I say to myself.

"You're turning art into an athletic event," he says sarcastically. "Mud wrestling!"

I push his shoulder out of my face, forgetting I have paint on my hand, and leave a brown blotch on his white T-shirt.

"Bite me," he says.

I swipe my paint-smeared hand across his cheek. I stare

at the brown streak on his face, shocked that I actually slapped him.

"Taylor!" says Mr. Lee. I freeze.

All I want is to turn back to my paper and slam down more paint. I don't want to talk or think. I'm *certainly* not going to apologize to the ape.

Mr. Lee comes over but doesn't say anything. We're like characters in a movie that's been put on pause.

Finally Mike shifts and speaks. "My fault, sir," he says. "I shouldn't have agitated an artist at work."

"You've got that right," says Mr. Lee, resting his hand on Mike's back. "Why don't you go to the bathroom and clean yourself up."

"No problem," says Mike.

I resume my paint slam. Mr. Lee hesitates beside me, then leans over and talks to RJ instead. Good man. I grab a blob of forest green and whack it down beside a smear of burnt sienna and a fistful of citrus yellow. I start to rotate my hands in a clockwise motion through the colors, anxiously looking for anything that might be a pattern or a shape. But nothing emerges, and the colors congeal into another wreck of mud.

A few minutes later Ebbie drops by the art room, as if this is visitors' day.

"Whoa," she says.

"Hi," I say.

"Feel good?" she asks.

"Not particularly. What are you doing out of class?"

"I needed to stretch. I passed Mike in the hall, and I thought I'd see if you were experimenting with other live canvases."

"I mistook him for a blank sheet."

"You'll be a legend someday," says Ebbie through her laughter. "See you at lunch!"

I turn back to my piece, *Study in Mud Number Ninety-seven.* I tear it, trash it, and prepare to attack my next innocent piece of paper.

"You've only got a few more minutes," says Mr. Lee from across the room. "Clean up. You can start a new piece tomorrow."

Before leaving, I go over to Mr. Lee. "Thanks for cutting me some slack."

"My pleasure," he says. "Sometimes you have to make a mess to get where you want to go. It'll come back."

"I've never lost anything before that's so hard to find," I mutter. I leave another mountain of crumpled paper in the garbage.

"Before you take off, Taylor," says Mr. Lee, following me to the door, "I've been wanting to ask you—how's your grandmother coming along?"

"I don't know," I say, surprised. "Not great."

"I'm sorry," he says. "That's a hard situation for you to face."

"Thanks," I say, pleased that he knows and embarrassed because I want to cry. "I've got to go."

This afternoon after school I go see Grams. Crushing a

corner of her bedspread in my hand, I cry and talk at the same time. "I hate art. I hate my work. It stinks. All I do now is create crud. Everything I've done since you got sick has been carted off to the dump. I'll have nothing new to submit to Salt Rock—nothing, and it's all because of *you*. How am I supposed to keep my act together when you're like this? Come back! I need you!"

If my old Grams were anywhere in there, she'd shake me until my brains shot out all over her room and splattered the whole stupid stinking nursing home. She wouldn't let me talk to her like this, or to myself. But this Grams doesn't do anything. She just sits and blinks.

I rip the macramé owl off the wall and stuff it in the wastepaper basket. *If I can't create beauty, at least I can destroy ugliness,* I think as I stalk out the door.

I'm so angry when I get home that I start smacking my stuffed animals around. As I'm shaking Ansel Adams, my old panda, he bursts apart, sending stuffing spilling out all over my comforter. Exhausted, I fall back on my bed, horrified at the person I'm becoming: someone who yells at grandmothers and beats up stuffed animals. This is not the girl Grams raised, the girl she named a star after.

I close my eyes and take a long breath in, then ride my exhale like a toboggan down a hill. I keep breathing slowly until a picture forms in my mind. I see a snowy meadow free of footprints. Making fresh tracks in new snow is easy and exciting. Walking into a new life without Grams next to me is going to be hard. It's going to take courage.

12

IF I CAN'T PAINT PAPER, then I'll paint myself. I start to wear paint as clothes. I encircle my bellybutton with gunmetal gray, creating the eye of a shark gliding past my stomach. Kate, who has a locker across from mine, is the first one to see it. "Cool," she says, and drags her friend Molly over for a viewing. I stop taking books out of my locker to let them admire my work.

The following day I paint the top of one arm and shoulder red and the other purple, with black slashes. I wear a black tank top, so it looks like I'm wearing a T-shirt with different-colored sleeves.

On Thursday I show up with half my face painted indigo blue. As I'm dropping off books in my locker, Mr. Debot taps me on the shoulder.

"Is this for some special project?" he asks, giving me the benefit of the doubt and, unwittingly, an explanation.

"Yes!" I nod enthusiastically.

"Drama?" he says.

"A play," I say, making an association with the word "drama."

"Ah."

"Open wide," I say, continuing my word-association game.

"Pardon?"

"Presidential," I say.

"Residential?"

"Housing development," I say.

Mr. Debot looks confused, glances at his watch, and says, "I'm late."

"White Rabbit," I respond. Oh, for a rabbit hole to push *him* down.

"Good luck with your project," he says, and quickly beats a retreat.

As I'm about to walk away, I'm intercepted by Ms. Shrum, the principal.

"Taylor Wickham, is that you?"

I smile widely and nod my head vigorously.

"Does the school know you're made up like this?" she says.

"Yes," I say, picturing the school's bricks granting their approval as I ran up the steps. "I just spoke with Mr. Debot."

"Oh," she says, apparently relieved. "He knows what this is about?"

"Absolutely."

"All right, then," says Ms. Shrum, and she waves me her blessing.

By the time Dad makes it home for an early dinner, I've washed the paint from my face, although the left side is still red from being scrubbed.

"So," says Dad, "how was your day?"

"OK," I say. "And yours?"

"Good," he says. "Anything interesting happen to you today?"

I shake my head no.

"Well, something unusual happened to me," he says. "I ran into Mr. Debot this afternoon."

I stare at the crumpled napkin in my lap, wondering where this is going.

"Do you know what he told me?"

I hate this kind of guessing game, so I decide not to play. I sit silently and wait for him to tell me.

"Apparently, you've been doing some off-canvas painting," he says, looking at my blotchy face. "What's up?"

"I was bored. I was out of paper. Whatever."

I look back down at my plate, suddenly fascinated by my mound of sticky white rice. I busy myself sculpting a face in the side of this mountain. Too bad I can't submit rice as art.

"Taylor?" says Dad. He's twisting his napkin around and around, turning it into a long snakelike shape. "something wrong?"

"Are you *kidding?*"

He looks confused.

"Grams is freaking me out. I don't have a mother now. We eat Chinese takeout and bean-sprout nightmares. *And* my artwork done a decent piece since Grams got going to be a total bust. Therefore, you wrong. A *lot* is wrong."

73

"I didn't realize you had so much weighing on you," says Dad, looking uncomfortable.

"Well, why would you? When have you ever really talked with me?" I mash the rice face into the plate.

Dad finishes wrecking his napkin and sets it aside. "I miss Grams, too," he says in a soft voice. A muscle in his jaw pulses in and out.

I pick up Dad's wrecked napkin and tie the white snaky thing into a knot. Grams was the thread that tied Dad and me together. With her vibrant personality and zest for life, she made actual conversations happen around this table.

"Is there anything I can do?" Dad asks.

"Make Grams better, make my art come back." I'm going to start either shouting or sobbing. "Talk about Mom."

"I would if I could, honey," he says, and starts playing with his lo mein.

Please say something, I say inside my head.

"Would you like to play tennis sometime?" he asks.

Earth to Dad. Like that'll help. Like I don't hate tennis. Doesn't he even know *that?* But all I say to him, in a flat, lifeless voice, is, "Sure, Dad."

"All right then," he says, as if something has been settled. "We'll *do* that."

He gets up and walks to the sink. I watch his back as e rinses his plate and wipes his hand across his eyes a uple of times.

"I'll finish up here," he says, his voice wavering.

I realize I'm not the only person on earth sad about life. I wish I'd get up and put my arm around Dad so we could be sad together. And even though I could do that—I could push back my chair, take five steps over to the sink, raise my arm up, and place it around his shoulders—I don't. I just don't know how.

"OK," I say instead. "Thanks. I'm going to my room."

On the way upstairs I scoop up yellow and green paint and a brush.

Tomorrow, to slog through the last day of school, I'll paint my feet.

13

AS SOON AS THE FINAL BELL RINGS, Ebbie and I bolt out of our last class. The trashcans are wobbling-full of notebooks and papers. Old sneakers, pencil stubs, rulers, and ripped books spill into the halls.

"Hey, Weird Girl," calls Ebbie, hauling stuff out of her locker. "Listen up, Chartreuse Feet. Do you want this?" She waves a paper we did on some ancient European treaty.

"Oh, yeah," I say, laughing. "Let's keep *that* forever!"

"It's *history*," she yells, crunching it into a ball and aiming for a trashcan.

I like Ebbie because she laughs a lot. We bonded when we had a laugh attack over our baggy uniforms in Ms.

Farley's gym class. Laughing keeps a rhythm going, like a drum in a rock band. I'll miss the beat of Ebbie over the summer. She'll be away at her grandmother's cottage up on Vancouver Island in Canada, a whole country away, until Labor Day.

"Now that school's over, you can concentrate on your pieces for Salt Rock," she says.

I wasn't expecting her to bring this up right now. I shake my head. "No."

"What do you mean, no? What are you sending?" she says, emptying her entire backpack into the trashcan.

I stare into my vacated locker and then at the unfinished collage hanging forlornly on the door.

"You *are* entering?" Ebbie asks. She comes over and stands right next to me. "Aren't you?"

I can't look at her. Dropping her backpack, she grabs my shoulders, turns me around, and sees the tears streaming down my face.

"I was so worried about you getting enough to eat and being depressed over Grams, I didn't stop to think you weren't getting work ready for Salt Rock."

"I haven't sent anything in, and I'm not going to."

"Has the deadline passed?" she asks. "Isn't there still time?"

"Not for me," I say. "It's in about two weeks."

"Why not for you?" says Ebbie, raking her hands through her short hair, making it stick up even more than usual.

"Everything I've done is crap."

"You must have *some* good stuff," she says. "What about from the fall, before Grams got sick?"

"It has to be work from January on. And my work's just not happening anymore, Eb."

"Not true," she shoots back, with a wry smile. "Look at your feet!"

"Aren't you late for your bus?" I say, turning her to face the hall clock.

"Oh, no!"

"Well, go," I say, pretending to shoo her away.

She stands staring at me for so long I almost forget we're in the middle of a conversation, and then she blurts out, "What did you have for dinner last night?"

"Not this again!"

"Come on, what did you have, Ant Girl?"

"I don't remember."

"Did you eat with your dad?"

"Yes."

"Picture your plate. What was on it?"

"I said I don't know, officer!" I respond as I salute. "Are you insane?"

"Who does your grocery shopping?" she asks, relentless.

"Grams, sir," I say.

"The last time anyone bought groceries at your house was *February?*"

"Kind of," I say. "We grab stuff."

"School's over," she says. "And I'm going away. Who's going to share their sandwiches with you while I'm gone?"

"I know how to make sandwiches," I say.

"Taylor, you have *got* to take care of yourself."

I shrug and nod OK, but I think of the laundry heap at the end of the hall near my room. It used to be a clothes hamper. Now it's a clothes *mountain,* on top of which I keep piling my dirty clothes, wishing that a fairy godmother would come along before I run out of under-wear, hoping that one morning I'll wake up and every-thing will be washed, folded, and put back in my drawers again, the way it was when Grams was here.

"Taylor," says Ebbie, "please take care of yourself. Promise me you'll eat. OK?"

I salute again.

"Say OK—and *mean* it."

"OK," I say.

"Mean it!"

"I solemnly swear that I, Taylor Wickham, will eat things."

"OK," she says, putting her arm around my shoulder and hugging me. "You're the coolest Ant Hole I've ever known. Take care of yourself!"

I grab her and hug her back hard.

"I am really sorry about your grandma and Salt Rock," she says softly into my hair. Eventually she steps away and picks up her backpack. "There's no computer at the cot-tage, so I'll snail-mail you. You'd better write back."

"Sure. You take care, too."

Now she has to run like crazy to catch her bus. I watch her bolt down the long hall with her backpack swinging like a pendulum from side to side. When she reaches the exit doors, she turns, and we wave to each other. It breaks my heart to see her vanish for a whole summer.

"Shit," I say to myself as I grab the cow chimes she gave me out of my locker.

"Taylor Wickham," booms The Voice, sounding like the God of Retribution.

"Have a good summer, Debot," I say, and slam the locker shut.

14

"LICORICE," I SAY. "Licorice, licorice, licorice."

I like this word. When I say it three times in a row, it sounds like wind passing through pine boughs.

Licorice was one of Grams's favorite words. She had lists of words she loved to say out loud, rolling them around on her tongue while she listened to their music. She wrote her favorites on strips of colored paper and kept them in an old cookie jar. *"Striped pipsissewa,"* she'd command, pulling one out of the jar. I'd repeat the word, and she'd drop it back into the jar, saying, "Marvelous! *What* a word!"

I pull down Grams's old jar and snatch out a handful of her words. *Bumblebee. Lollygag. Meander. Plum.* Licorice,

licorice, licorice. Perhaps I'll just sit around all summer twirling words on my tongue.

The last day of school usually feels like the end of a jail term, and all I want to do is shout, "Free at last!" School's like a huge textbook I'm forced to trudge through for ten long months every year, and June is the last page of the last chapter, when I get to slam the book shut. It's all over, and it's just beginning. I used to feel reborn as I stepped into the first days of summer, those lush green days of boundless possibilities. But this summer looks like it's going to be one long, empty road—a thousand miles of nothing until September. I'll probably go two whole months without talking to anyone, or maybe I'll just say "Licorice." Dad's always working. Grams is a ghost of herself. I could collapse on the floor in her room at the Golden Edges chanting, "Licorice, licorice, licorice," and she wouldn't hear or care.

I wish I'd lined up a job to keep my mind off the pain of Grams being gone and my inability to create one single satisfying image. Being sad puts brakes on my brain. The whole summer is waiting to be lived, but I'm not likely to wrap my arms around it and squeeze the juice out of each day.

"No job?" says Dad, when I mention how boring this summer's going to be. "How about Harrington's snack bar down near the beach?"

"I want to spend my time visiting Grams," I lie.

I hate going to see Grams. Whenever I walk into the

Golden Edges, I feel like a small child being shoved into a haunted house. I hate how I feel when I go. I hate how I feel when I don't go.

"Licoricelicoricelicorice," I say quickly and too loudly.

Dad looks confused, picks up a box of licorice from the counter, and offers it to me. I shake my head.

"*Licorice* is one of Grams's favorite words," he says, looking like he just figured out a Zen koan.

"It was," I say.

"I imagine it still is," says Dad.

"Whatever."

When Dad leaves for work, I sit out on the porch staring vacantly at a cloudless sky. I glance at Bears's house and idly wonder what he's going to do now that school's over. When we were little, we hung out every second of our lives, especially in the summer. We wore identical T-shirts. We used the same expressions. I don't have a clue what he thinks anymore, but I smile, remembering the bugs in the prom punch.

Suddenly a flock of starlings, crackling with chatter, swoop into the silver maple. Grams taught me to identify every type of bird that landed in our yard and to recognize their calls. She bought seeds for them right through the summer, so it seemed there were always a billion birds soaring around our house. As she poured seeds into the feeder, she'd proclaim, "The café's open. The seeds are fresh, so fly on in." When I was little, I assumed the birds heard and understood. When I got older, and she'd talk to birds in front of my friends, I wanted to bag her and drag her inside. "She's completely insane," I'd say, "but it's not hereditary!"

Grams taught me lots of life stuff. "Figure out who you are before you pull on shoes," she once told me. "No use buckling up sandals when what you really want to do is run!" But she never taught me what to do if she got old and lost . . . can't come back . . . gone.

I wander around trying to decide what to wear on this first morning of my first long summer alone. *Who am I today?* Then I take the long way over to see Grams, but that's all I do. I see her. I don't know if she sees me. I don't even *try* to get a conversation going.

After a few minutes I get up to go. I turn in the doorway and say, "Licorice."

Grams looks right at me. "Good afternoon," she says, even though it's still morning.

My heart does a triple back flip. "I'm sorry about what I said the other day," I tell her, stepping back into the room. "I—"

"Jimmy brought roses," she says, interrupting me. "And raspberries."

"Who's Jimmy?" I say, completely frustrated that Grams is off in her fantasy world again.

She waves toward her bureau. There's a fresh bouquet of roses in a vase! I feel like I'm in her dream, dreaming what she's seeing. Beside the roses is a little basket. When

I go over and peek inside, there are red stains on the bottom and two squashed raspberries.

"Grams?" I say softly, turning back to her. "Who is Jimmy?"

But she's already fallen asleep again, looking like an empty clump of clothes. I want to shake her. I want to shout, "Give me back my Grams!" This old lady is swallowing my Grams.

I'm tiptoeing back toward the door again when she opens her eyes and says, "Roses."

"We should all get them," I say back.

"Mmm," she mutters, falling back asleep.

"Striped pipsissewa," I answer, as her head lolls to the side.

I run back to the house, too dried up inside to cry. The rest of the day's a blur. I'm losing whole days worrying over something I can't do anything about.

In the late afternoon our mail carrier, Dave, knocks on the door. When I open it he says, "How's your grandmother?"

"I don't know," I say.

Dave raises his eyebrows and tilts his head.

"Sometimes she's almost there, but mostly she isn't."

"Ah," he says. "It's hard, isn't it?"

"Yeah," I say.

"She's a great lady. I miss her." We stand on the stoop in silence for a few seconds. "Well," he finally says, "hang in there." He hands me our mail and I watch him start back down the path.

"*Was* a great lady," I call.

Dave turns and looks at me. "Is," he calls back. "She still is."

15

I SLIP DOWNSTAIRS AND SIT on the third step while Dad rummages around in the front hall, getting ready for work.

"Are you ever going to just be home?" I ask, aware that I'm about to spend the whole summer practically alone in our empty house.

"What does that mean?" he says, struggling to do his tie and frowning either at it or at me.

"We never spend time together."

"I didn't know you paid any attention to whether I'm here or not."

"I notice," I say. "I learned to tell time just so I could see for myself when you were coming home. So I could meet you at the corner, because I couldn't wait."

"That's right. I'd forgotten that. I didn't realize you still notice when I get home, unless I'm late with dinner."

"Well, I do, OK? I'm not going to run to the corner to meet my daddy now, but I still like knowing you're home."

"It's good to know," he says. He stops fiddling with his

tie and smiles to himself, then turns and checks himself in the hall mirror. I get up, stand beside him, and look at both of us in the mirror.

"Grams talks a lot about roses," I say to his reflection.

Now we're both looking at each other and ourselves in the mirror.

"Grams loves roses," he says. "That's why she chose Rose for your middle name. And because it's hers, too."

"*Grams* chose my middle name?"

"I thought you knew that," says Dad, turning to look at the real me. "I'm surprised she didn't tell you. I thought she told you everything there was to tell."

"Tell me now, Dad. I want to know these kinds of stories."

"Well, your mom loved Grams. Her own mother, your other grandmother, seemed to have a list of everything your mom ever did wrong. Grams, as you know, celebrates people, and your mom ate it up. When she was pregnant with you, she wanted to honor Grams, so she asked her to give you your middle name. Grams decided to share hers with you, so that's how you became a Rose, too."

"That's cool," I say. "I thought Mom named me. I wish you'd tell me more things like this."

"I'll try to think of some," he says, kissing my forehead. "I'm off, sweetie."

Last year I loved the sound of the click of the door when the last person left. The moment after that click was a most satisfying silence. Now I dread it. After the door closes behind Dad, the air in the house feels tight. As I watch him walking to the car, he suddenly turns around, as if he senses me watching him, smiles, and blows me a kiss.

What do Dad and I know about each other? Not much. I don't even know how he feels about his own mother fading away. And he doesn't know I'm lonely and weirded out in the house now.

I need to talk to someone. I pick up the phone and punch in Ebbie's number. Maybe she hasn't left.

"Hi, it's Taylor," I say when her mother answers the phone. "Is Ebbie there?" I catch myself listening to my own voice. With Grams's humming, singing, and chatting, it was rarely quiet in the kitchen. The air was always full of her sounds.

"Oh, Taylor, honey, she left for Vancouver Island already."

"OK," I say. "Well, when you talk to her, please tell her I say hi. Bye."

Her mother probably won't remember to tell her I called. She once forgot her youngest kid, Geordie, at the Star store.

I think of calling Mindy, even though we're so different now. It's like we boarded different boats: She landed in France, and I sailed off to New Zealand or someplace equally far away. We don't know what to say to each other anymore, almost as if we speak different languages.

As I'm thinking all this, I punch in Mindy's number anyway. When she picks up, I don't know what to say. She has to say hello twice.

"Hi, Mindy. It's Taylor," I finally manage to mumble, suddenly feeling shy.

"Taylor?"

"Yeah."

"Is everything OK?"

"Yeah, well, I don't know. What do you mean?"

"I don't know. Last time we talked was before the prom. How did your date with Mike go?" she says.

"I pushed him into the bushes."

"Oh, good," she says. "So . . ."

"So," I say, feeling lost. "How's your aunt Min?"

"OK, I guess. It's weird seeing her in there."

"I know it," I say. "I hate Grams being there."

Then we're not talking. Just breathing into our phones.

"OK. Well," I say, my voice trailing off.

"Yup."

"Take care," I say.

"Yeah," she says. "You, too. I'm glad you're OK and everything."

"What are you talking about?"

"Whoops, there's my mom. I've got to go, Taylor."

"Sure. See you."

I meander into my room, plunk myself down on the bed with a sketchbook, and drag a pencil across a page. My lines resemble skid marks on a gym floor. I can see outlines through a mist, but I can't reach any concrete ideas. I shove the sketchbook off my lap so hard it shoots across the room and bangs into the dresser with a thud. Grams always said to stop and figure out how I feel—sad, angry, or scared, stuff like that. I sit still for a moment and really try to concentrate. But my emotions are so choppy and blurred, they're like a storm at sea. If I felt my feelings full force, I might drown.

16

I SPENT HOURS IN THE PARK every summer as a kid, but I haven't been to the park in a long time. I decide to get on my bike and take a spin over there.

"Hey!" Bears calls as I pedal down the driveway. "Wait!"

I come to a stop in front of his stoop.

"How's life?" he says.

"It sucks."

"Grams?"

"Yeah."

"I miss her. It feels different not having Grams right next door."

"Really?" I say.

"Yeah. She was always so lively, I used to think her energy could generate electricity for the whole neighborhood. I miss hearing her sing and seeing her dance that weird jig in the garden. I miss hanging out and talking to her."

"There's nothing lively about her now. She's mostly a noodle," I say bluntly.

"It's not her fault, T," he says.

"I never said it was."

"But did you think it?" says Bears, winking at me.

We used to say that all the time. One of us would say something like, "I never said you were dumb." And then the other would say, "Yeah, but did you think it?" It's amazing that even though we haven't been tight for the past few years, we seem to be sliding into an easy back-and-forth.

"Do you remember how Grams used to say, 'If you want to be close, you have to let each other in'?" he continues. "'You can't throw words into the air and hide behind them, not if you want to dance with someone and know them deep.' She wanted us to say what was bugging us. She always encouraged us to speak our minds."

"I remember," I say defensively.

"Listen, T, if you want to talk about Grams, I'm here for you."

"She weirds me out," I say softly, embarrassed at having snapped at him.

"I know, it's hard to see her just sitting and staring at life instead of racing around 'smack in the middle of it,'" says Bears, smiling at the memory of another Grams expression.

"Have you been to see her?" I ask, surprised. I hadn't thought of anyone visiting Grams but Dad and me.

"What do you think?" he says, frowning at me. "*Of course* I've been to see her!"

Even though we're falling back into conversation, we're edgy. I don't remember Bears and me snapping at each other like this, going from hard to soft and back. And of course he'd go visit Grams. He's spent almost as much time with Grams as I have; he was over constantly. Grams called him her honorary grandson. I've been too wrapped up in my own pain to consider anyone else's feelings but my own.

"I'm so sorry, Bears. I should've known you wouldn't abandon Grams." But my apology fails to smooth out his frown. "Are you angry about anything else?"

"Yeah," he says. "I am."

"Are you going to tell me or do I have to guess?"

Bears shakes his head at my impatience. "Finding Grams like that was hard for me, too, you know," he says. "Seeing her lying there on the floor still plays back in my head, and it hurts to think about. I need to talk about it, and I think you do, too. But when I try to talk with you, you blow me off."

"Not true," I interrupt, despite knowing that it's absolutely true.

"When's the last time you came over or stopped to talk?" he asks.

We haven't really talked since the beginning of ninth grade.

Bears scratches his elbow. "I miss hanging out," he says slowly.

"We hang out," I say pointlessly. "OK, maybe not for a while, but you could have tried."

I know I should be apologizing, but I keep arguing. It's less embarrassing than admitting I've been a jerk.

"I wasn't going to force you to stay friends," says Bears.

I start scraping mud off the top of my front fender.

"I kept coming over to your house," he continues. "But you were always busy, so eventually I stopped. You never came over to my house, called, or even returned my calls."

"I didn't really notice," I say. "It just happened."

"Well, *I* noticed," says Bears, coming off his porch to stand next to me. "I notice when my friends stop noticing me." He takes a tennis ball out of his pocket and starts tossing it up in the air.

"I said that wrong," I say, wishing I could erase his hurt feelings like chalk off a board. Bears was so familiar, so much a part of my life, that I didn't stop to think how he'd feel when I started hanging out with new people. I picked him out of my life, as if he meant nothing more than an outfit I didn't feel like wearing for a while.

"I'm sorry," I say finally. "I know 'sorry' doesn't make up for it, but I mean it."

"Thanks," he says, backing up and tossing me the ball.

We play catch until I miss the ball and he runs across the lawn after it.

"Are you staying on the island this summer?" he says as he brings it back.

"Yeah," I say. "You?"

Sun lights his hair from behind as he says, "Yes, lifeguarding down at the beach."

I move my bike back and forth like a pendulum, letting the warm metal brush my legs. We just kind of breathe in and out, not talking, not looking at each other. I feel kind of shy as I say, "Let's hang out this summer."

Bears agrees. The way he looks at me makes me feel like we've just met each other. The only thing I can think of to say is, "Did you bug the ice cubes at the prom?"

Bears laughs and says, "What do *you* think?"

"I don't know." I shift my bike against my left leg and squeeze the handlebars. "Did you?"

He just smiles. "Where are you going?"

"The park," I say. "Are you going to tell me?"

"Nope."

"OK. Well, see ya." I turn my bike around.

"Definitely. Thanks for stopping. It was good to talk."

I see his smile in my mind the whole way to the park.

When I arrive, I wander over to the willows. A little boy jumps off a low branch, skirts around me, and runs off to the swings. The way he runs off reminds me of when I was small and avoided the big kids. It's weird *being* the big kid.

I've been climbing these trees since I was about six. Today I climb higher than I've ever gone, find a comfortable spot, and freeze, becoming a great blue heron. I love watching those long-legged birds stand in shallow water, waiting to spot an unsuspecting fish. They stand as still as statues, as though they aren't in their bodies anymore but in a restful somewhere-else-place, balancing on one leg, completely still, like a piece of sky above the water.

I stay up in the tree until I hear a mother calling her children in for lunch. I pretend she's *my* mother, and I make my way home, too.

17

WHILE I WASH MY HAIR, loose strands wind around my fingers. Instead of letting the force of the water wash them down the drain, I drape them on the shower wall, making patterns on the tile. Curls become rounded butts, the outline of a breast, a piece of fruit. As I rinse out the shampoo, I watch the designs the suds make as they swirl around the drain and disappear.

Then I curl up in the most comforting place in the world, the porch swing. I pick up a book on the life of Michelangelo and start reading from where I'd left off the day before.

"Hey!" says Bears as he bounds up the porch steps carrying a Frisbee.

"Horses," I say back without thinking.

"What's up?" he asks.

I'm momentarily too absorbed in the Italian Renaissance to reply right away.

"Hey, girl with the wet head!" he says, leaning over and gently pulling a hunk of my hair.

I pat the seat beside me, and Bears flops down, joggling the swing. Our hips touch like they have a thousand times. I never noticed it before, but now I do. I feel embarrassed, like I should shift away or go and sit on the steps.

Bears scans the cover of my book and then points to my easel, which is leaning against the house. "Your easel—it's folded up," he says, smacking a beat on his knee with his Frisbee.

"Yes," I say.

"I never even knew it *could* fold up," he says, teasing me, knowing that from the first warm day on I'm usually out here painting.

I ignore this, grab a section of my hair, and begin braiding it.

When I'm finished, Bears tugs on the braid and says, "I know it's hell having Grams slip away, but you have to hold on to your art, T."

He stands up, scoops up a tube of paint from under the windowsill, and holds it out to me. "Crimson lake— isn't this your favorite color?" he says, reading the side of the tube.

"Once," I say, grabbing the tube. I pitch it off the porch and into the zinnias.

"OK, so it's not your favorite anymore," he says. "Hey, I just realized—I never found out what's up with Salt Rock."

Those two words, "salt" and "rock," pave my face like asphalt.

"I'm working on it," I say, hoping he'll drop the subject.

"Hey," says Bears, knocking my arm. "Come play Frisbee with me."

I follow him out to the grass. We throw the Frisbee back and forth to each other until I sail it over the fence and into his yard.

"Let's have lemonade," I say.

"Great."

When we're settled on the swing again, Bears says, "I wish Grams was in the kitchen humming to herself, about to bring out the blue pitcher and ask if we want more."

I weave my fingers together, like I used to do a long time ago for the finger game "Here is the church," and watch my knuckles turn white. I feel tears I don't want Bears to see. I sit perfectly still so as not to jiggle them out of my eyes.

"I wish she were coming home," he says. "I miss her."

"And I wish you'd stop talking about Grams, because she's not coming home, she's never coming home, and wishing won't bring her back or make things better."

"No, she's not," says Bears, his voice breaking and his face crumbling.

After a long pause he continues, "Do you and your dad ever talk about what's happening with Grams?"

"No, Bears, we don't. Since when have Dad and I ever communicated about anything important? Now will you please talk about something else!"

Bears is quiet for a long time, and then he says, "She's just stuck inside an old body. It's just what is."

"Tell it to the screen door," I say, scrambling up and running inside. I slam the door and stand in the kitchen feeling flat as paper.

"Let me know if you want to go see Grams together. Or talk," says Bears, peering through the wire mesh.

"I don't," I say.

I watch him walk back through the garden gate to his house. "I'm a mess," I say to the tiles on the floor.

18

MY BREATH IS HOT AND MY tears spill onto my pillow. I don't stop sobbing for a long time. Eventually I come up for air, and when I roll over, Mai Ling thunks off the bed. I lean down to scoop her up, and I hear the porch swing creaking. Such a sweet sound. So many nights after Grams said good night to me, she'd go down and glide by herself.

The comforting sound of the song of the swing would drift in my window and lull me to sleep.

Thinking Bears must have come back, I roll off my bed and creep downstairs. I push open the screen door, ready to apologize for being so edgy, and I'm completely taken by surprise to see Mike.

"Hi," he says. "I knocked, but no one came. I kind of heard something inside, though, so I thought I'd wait."

"Why?" I say. "What are you doing here?"

"Do you want to go down to Harrington's for ice cream?"

"Are you kidding?"

"Why would I be kidding?"

I'm saying the dumbest things, and I don't know why.

"OK," I say. "Sure, let me grab my sandals."

I can't believe I said yes. I wish I could rewind.

As we walk around to the front of the house, Bears is shooting hoops in his driveway.

"Nice," calls Mike as Bears sinks a long jump shot. Bears gives us a quick wave, scoops up the ball, and dribbles toward the basket again.

"So," I say, turning to Mike. "What *are* you doing in my neighborhood?"

"I'm doing carpentry jobs around town. In fact, I'm starting on your back porch next weekend."

"Our porch? You're kidding!" I say.

"No, once again I'm not kidding. I came over to check

it out, measure and stuff. That's why I was at your place. Are you around this summer?"

"No," I say. "I won't be here." What I mean is, *No, I don't want to hang around with you.*

"Where are you going?"

"Ebbie's grandmother's," I lie.

"Where's that?"

"Up north. Canada."

"Soon?" he says.

"Yes. No. I'm not sure."

We arrive at Harrington's. I've never been less hungry.

"What do you want?" asks Mike, leaning on the freezer case and staring at the flavors.

"I had a huge bowl of cereal right before you came," I lie again.

I'm lying about everything. It's like a disease, or a spell. If he asks me if I want to strip naked and have him lick ice cream off my body, I'll have to say yes. Or if he asks if I want fifty thousand dollars, I'll have to say no.

He shrugs and orders a chocolate ripple sundae.

"Want to walk down to the beach?" he asks, grabbing his ice cream and a wad of napkins.

Of course I say yes, because of the lying spell.

As we walk, I realize I know nothing about Mike. Most of our relationship consists of him teasing me or asking me out, and me giving sarcastic replies. I have no idea how to be normal with this guy. I feel like I'm walking on top of crusty snow, hoping to not fall through. I felt more comfortable when I hated him.

Mike sits down on a rock, and I sink down on the sand.

"When I see you at school, you're funny and comfortable with other people," he says. "But with me, you're cold and sharp. Did I do something to bug you? I mean, something other than ask you out a couple of hundred times?"

"You knocked RJ into the lockers once," I say immediately.

"What?" he says.

I'm surprised I've just blurted this out. Apparently, the lying spell has been broken.

"Back in ninth grade," I say, feeling stupid as I say it.

"Back in ninth grade?" he says. "You're pissed at me for something I did in *ninth grade?*"

"Yes," I say hesitantly.

"There's got to be something else," he says, "or you're nuts."

"You're crude about breasts," I say. The spell has reversed. Suddenly, not only can I not lie, I have to say the exact, specific truth!

Mike stops scooping ice cream out of the plastic bowl and stares at me. He glances down toward my breasts and then quickly looks away.

"I've got to go," he says. "Have a good time at your grandmother's."

"It's Ebbie's grandmother," I say.

"Yeah, OK. Whatever," he says, and he takes off.

If he'd stayed, I might have told him I'm not really going to Ebbie's grandmother's, maybe even that my own grandmother is . . . dying. But he didn't stay. And now I'm going to get caught in a stupid lie and feel ridiculous the next time I see him. Which is apparently going to be at my own house. Next week.

I watch Mike walk down the beach. A lot of girls wave to him and he stops to talk to some of them. I keep watching until he blends in with everyone else in the distance.

19

Thursday, June 12

> *Alessa stares at the trees outside her window.*
> *Leaves flutter like feeding birds.*
> *Alma across the hall sits fascinated or dead*
> *in front of a television.*
> *Alessa does the same with her window.*
> *She's sailing on air*
> *shifting wherever it drifts*
> *her mind as thin as a wisp.*

I look up from my poem to glance at Grams, who's sitting in a wheelchair by the window. She didn't turn around when I said her name, so I quietly pulled a chair up right next to her. I tried sketching, but it looked like bird feet in dirt. Better than mud, I guess, but I decided to write instead.

I poke my nose with the end of my pencil, enjoying the smell of the new pink eraser. That scent brings back the excitement of the first day of grade school, when I'd wear a brand-new outfit and gulp down breakfast, thrilled to start the year. I didn't feel sad that summer was ending, just eager to meet my new teacher and sit at my new desk. It was on that first day that Grams always waved a bubble-gum pink eraser under my nose at breakfast and announced, "Don't be afraid to make lots of mistakes, honey—that's what erasers are for."

I look around Grams's room, wondering what it feels like to be Grams now. I wrote a piece about everything being packed up and Grams just waiting to die. I hope that's not right, that she's in her own fantasy world, maybe a Chagall-like dreamy place.

I'm startled out of my reverie when Grams suddenly pitches forward and stares at her shoes. I want to readjust her as if she's one of my dolls, sit her up and face her toward the window again, but I'm afraid to touch her. She used to feel solid and strong; lately when I hug her, she feels like play dough, as though she'll cave in if I touch her too hard. I want to talk with her about the color of the sky today, the shapes of the clouds, the way the trees are dancing in the wind; to ask her the name of the bird that lands on a branch and fluffs its wings. But I think, *What's the point?* and drop my head on the windowsill and cry.

I cry until the room fills with water and my chair floats out the window, carrying me down the street to Puget Sound. When I finally come back to the Golden Edges, I'm startled to feel the unexpected pressure of Grams's hand on my arm. I love this hand I'm staring at, the veins riding along the back of it and disappearing into her knuckles, the shape of her slender fingers. I gaze up into her face, but only her hand is with me. Her eyes are far off in another place. I kiss the back of her hand, give it three squeezes—our code for *I love you*—place it in her lap, and leave. That's the sweetest thing I've done for Grams in a long time.

As I'm walking toward the exit, I hear muffled noises coming from inside a closet and wonder if Alma has wandered off and locked herself in. I open the door slowly, so that if it is Alma and she's leaning on it, she won't fall out.

"What the . . . who are *you?*" squeals a girl in a candy-striped uniform, spinning around and squirming out of the grasp of a pair of arms.

"Oops, excuse me," I say.

"Hey, T!"

"Bears?"

"The one and only," says Bears.

As my eyes adjust to the dim light of the closet, I realize that the volunteer in there with him is the perfect girl from the prom. Their faces are red, and I'm sure mine is, too. I'd turn and leave, but I can't make my hand let go of the doorknob. I wish I'd stop staring at them.

"T, how about letting us out before we freak out someone's grandpa," quips Bears, breaking my trance and restoring the use of my hand.

"This is a closet," I say lamely as Closet Girl adjusts her uniform, trying to hide the hickey on her neck.

"We know," Bears answers calmly. "But it's one that isn't used very often . . . by the staff."

"Oh," I mumble, feeling ridiculous. Then I get spitting-mean. "So this is why you come to see Grams," I hiss at Bears, knowing it's not true but unable to control my anger and confusion. "You don't care about Grams. You just want to neck with a fake nurse!"

I spin around and take off for the street at ninety miles an hour. Mr. Eliot, who's shuffling out into the hall, pauses in his doorway just in the nick of time. A second later and I'd have flattened the old geezer right into the linoleum.

I keep up the same pace all the way home and arrive sweaty and steaming. I grab a piece of charcoal and try sketching something worth using up paper for, riding the energy of my anger. But I'm crying and the paper is getting wet and tearing, smearing the black lines I've scribbled on the page. I drew better pictures when I was just learning how to hold a crayon.

Later I hear Dad answer a knock at the back door.

"It's Barry," Dad calls up to me.

Coming into the kitchen, I find Bears leaning against the sink, a pair of Coke cans in his hand. "Let's go out on the porch," he says, holding the screen door open for me.

"So let's go see Grams together sometime," he says.

"You said that already, the last time you came over," I shoot right back, still carrying the confusion of catching Bears making out with Closet Girl. "But I don't remember getting any calls from you."

"You just stopped paying attention to any of my calls, Taylor. But here I am, and I'm asking you again if you want to visit Grams with me. I didn't think it would be such a difficult idea for you to consider. What is up with you?"

Bears is sitting on the porch floor with his back against the wall of the house and I'm sitting cross-legged on the swing, just like we used to do. We sit in silence for a while, making slurping sounds as we sip our sodas. This feels like it could be old times, but it's not.

"I'm sorry, OK? I'd like to go see Grams with you."

"OK," he says.

"So who's Closet Girl?" I ask.

"Her name is Evelyn, and she just moved here from Seattle. I met her last year over at the Folk Life festival."

"She sure got involved with the community fast."

Bears laughs. "Did you have a good time with Mike yesterday?" he asks, turning the tables on me.

"Not as good as your time in the closet," I counter.

Bears stares at his soda can and tries again. "How was your date with Mike?"

"It wasn't a date," I say.

"What was it?"

"A fig," I say sarcastically.

"A what?"

"Date, fig. Get it?"

Bears groans.

"Dad hired him to fix the porch," I say quickly. "He came over to figure out an estimate, not for a date with me."

"Right."

"It's true," I insist.

"He's liked you forever," says Bears. "You know that."

"He's *bugged* me forever. I know *that.*"

"Same thing."

I pick up a twig that's blown onto the swing and flick it at Bears.

"You didn't look that bugged about being with him," he says.

"You didn't look at all bugged to be making out with Closet Girl," I hiss back.

"You are so charged up. What's with you?" says Bears, tilting his head and looking cute as he gazes quizzically up at me.

I look at him and wonder why no one I know seems the same anymore. I just walked the beach with Mike and found out I don't really hate him. I guess I disliked him for so long, it was eventually more like a habit than something I chose. And then I unearth Bears in a closet and discover that I get pissed off seeing him kiss some girl I don't even know. Everyone's different, even me.

"Forget it," I say to Bears. "I think it's great you have someone. I don't know why I reacted like that. I mean, it's not like . . . well, I'm sorry, OK?"

"Yeah," says Bears. "It's OK, I said that already. But who sounds jealous now?"

He stretches, grabs both our empty cans, and carries them into the kitchen. I hear the *crink* of the cans landing in the recycling bin. He still knows the routine around here. That's one thing that hasn't changed.

"About going to see Grams together," Bears says as he comes out.

"Yeah," I say, still feeling like biting the head off a snake. "That's why you came over, isn't it?"

"Yes, *and* to talk. So, I'd like to do that. If you're up for it, let me know."

He takes off without waiting for a reply, walking with his hands shoved into his pockets. He glances around the garden, stopping beside Grams's red Traviata roses to watch a hummingbird swoop by. Sunlight catches its ruby throat, and Bears turns to me and points. We catch each other's eye and I feel his smile shoot down my entire body.

20

IT'S MORNING, AND I LIE IN BED thinking of Bears. Images of him play through my mind as if I'm seeing him in a movie. Bears leaning against the porch railing with the sun spinning his hair gold; his thigh brushing mine as we sit on the swing together; his crooked smile. But then the scene shifts, and I see him with his arms wrapped around the candy-striped nurse and my hand frozen on the doorknob.

I feel my face stiffen when I think of Closet Girl. I lean over, grab my hand mirror, and stare at myself. The way my reflection stares back at me, frozen and hard, suddenly reminds me of a day I spent with Mindy last autumn.

Although we had drifted away from each other, Mindy and I had been assigned a joint social studies project about the differences between women who were mothers and women who chose not to have kids. We decided to hang out at the playground and do some live research on mothers.

"They look like they might have been cool once, but definitely not now," I said, checking out the moms slumped on picnic benches, leaning on slides, or staring vacantly as they pushed swings. "These women look sucked dry."

"*Totally,*" said Mindy.

We strolled behind the mothers pushing toddlers on swings, trolling for snippets of dialogue, but after ten minutes of listening to Lesley's reaction to organic applesauce, some new juice cup that doesn't drip, and the theory and practice of toilet training, we decided to skip our fieldwork. We took off for a bench on the other side of the park.

"It's like their brains blooped out along with their babies," I said. "Do you think they were ever vital or interesting? How many of them wish they'd had an abortion? . . . Let's ask them!" I said, joking around.

Mindy, who'd been digging the toe of her sneaker into the grass and boring a hole, suddenly swore and stood up.

"Sex and then babies," I went on, standing up beside her. I was feeling silly and on a roll. "Guys are dangerous. They terrify me, but I *want* one!" I was hoping to make Mindy laugh.

"I'm not working on this project anymore," she said sullenly. Her face was frozen, as sharp and hard as rock. "Get another partner."

I drift back to sleep thinking about Mindy and babies, Bears and his gold hair, and it all weaves into a surrealistic dream. I'm flying on the back of a purple baby with curly gold hair, watching Mindy in a long white gown falling out of a blue tree. Guitars with red roses in place of strings slide by, followed by a flock of multicolored birds flying upside down underneath them. If I can't paint, at least I can have Chagall dreams, I think, as the purple baby spreads out magenta wings and swoops down to break Mindy's fall.

Floating toward the outer edge of awake, I hear a bird trying to fly through my window, crashing against the glass again and again. I pull myself out of my reverie and rush to open the window, shouting, *"Stop!"*

"It's about time," says Bears, smiling up at me. "I was going to switch from pebbles to boulders."

"What?" I yell, trying to clear my head. I can't believe I'm shouting at Bears again. It seems like every time I see him, I end up barking like a mad dog on a short leash.

"Are you *ever* going to talk normally to me, or are you just going to yell at me for the rest of your sorry life?" he asks.

"Just a minute!" I say, leaning out my window and finally grinning at him. *"I'll be right down!"*

I brush my teeth, get my hair out of shock, and put in a pair of long jade-beaded earrings with tiny amethyst stars on the ends, liking the way they lightly kiss my cheeks when I turn my head.

Bears is sitting in the sun on the back step, singing quietly and tapping his fingers on his knees. I stop inside the door for a moment, tasting the pleasure of seeing the sweet look of concentration on his face. Finally, I swing the door open and let him know I'm here. "Signaling aliens?" I quip, covering up my sudden sense of shyness.

"No, I'm practicing fingerpicking."

"Practicing *what?*" I say.

"I'm practicing different fingerpicking patterns for the guitar," he says patiently.

"That's so weird. I just dreamed about guitars, but they had flowers instead of strings." I sit down next to him and watch his fingers tap a series of figures, as if he's playing piano on his knee. "Since when do you play guitar?"

"It's been almost two years, T—there are lots of new things in my life."

"Yeah, like kissing in closets."

Bears ignores me and places his hand on my thigh, continuing the finger pattern on my knee.

"All the new stuff in *my* life is bad," I sigh. With his fingers lightly strumming my skin, I'm having a hard time concentrating on the conversation.

Bears stops his finger patterns and caresses my cheek with the backs of his fingers. "Let's go see Grams together, right now," he says.

"No," I say in a slightly panicky voice. "I just went yesterday."

"Come on, T," he says, coaxing me. "Come on." It feels good to hear him call me "T" again.

He helps me up, and off we go.

Our arms brush against each other as he holds the heavy door open for me, and the heat of that touch stays with me as we walk down the cool hall toward Grams's room. A way-too-smiley nurse is pushing a cart down the corridor. "Your grandmother is in the lounge watching television," she says.

"She's doing *what?*" I shout.

"What's wrong?" asks Bears.

"Grams is in the TV room!"

"So?"

"Grams doesn't watch TV, Bears. She *hates* the idiot box."

Bears looks at me with his head tipped to the side like a puppy. "Life changes, T. People shift."

"I know!" I say, my voice rising. "But not Grams!"

I run down the hall and spot the back of Grams's head in a wheelchair parked in front of the TV. I dodge the nurse who's handing out cookies, lean down, and tell Grams, "It's OK, I'm here. I'll save you," as if I'm a superhero and life is this simple. I free the brake on her chair and spin her around so fast that she tilts way over. I speed past Bears toward the front doors like we're in some kind of wheelchair derby.

"Are you kidnapping her?" he calls, sounding concerned and running to catch up.

"Open the doors!" I shout dramatically.

"What are we doing?" he asks, holding the doors wide open.

I shove Grams's chair out into the sunlight and stop. I'd forgotten about the steps leading up to this place. There's nowhere else to wheel her.

"Hey, Grams," says Bears, leaning over and smiling at her. "Are you OK?"

"Roses," she says, and smiles at the pink Queen Elizabeth roses twining up the trellis beside the front door. Bears leans over and picks one, pries off the thorns, and presents it to her. She doesn't reach for it. He holds it under her nose, but she doesn't sniff.

I burst into tears, push the brake into place, and race home, leaving Bears to tend to Grams.

About thirty minutes later Bears is throwing dirt clods at my window. I ignore his signal for as long as it takes me to dry my tears.

"What?" I finally shout. "Don't you knock on doors anymore?"

He just looks up at me, waving me down, holding a pink rose in his other hand.

I go down the stairs and out onto the porch.

"That was a dumb thing to do," he says.

I stand with my arms crossed tightly against my chest.

"Here," he says, handing me the rose.

"Hey!" I yell as he walks away.

He doesn't even slow down.

"Who the hell do you think you are?" I shout. "What do you know about losing someone you love?"

But Bears has disappeared.

As I turn to go into the house, I notice that Grams's forget-me-nots are all tangled up with weeds. I lean over to free a few and wind up yanking out weeds by the fistful, until the bed around the plants is completely cleared. When I go back into the kitchen, my hands are full of green stains and dirt, just like Grams's hands used to be after she had gardened.

21

I'VE CALLED EBBIE'S GRANDMOTHER'S house three times, but no one's ever there, and apparently her grandmother doesn't believe in answering machines.

I'm holding the phone after another failed attempt when it rings.

"Just checking to see if you'll be there tomorrow so I can start on the porch," Mike says when I answer.

"Why do I have to be here?" I ask. "The porch is outside. Come whenever you want to."

"Right," he says. "Just checking."

"OK, well—that's nice of you, I guess," I say.

"See you soon."

"OK," I say. "Bye."

What was that about?

Being normal with Mike and furious with Bears makes my stomach hurt. I realize that I actually want to see more of Mike, and that freaks me out. As for Bears, I'm like a surprise grab bag around him. I never know what feelings will spill out when he shows up.

I return to the safety of my room and pace, pausing at the window every third or fourth lap to shoot a glance at

Bears's window. I remind myself of a wolf I once saw in a zoo. The whole time I watched, she paced the same oval over and over. If I keep circling like this, I'll wear a rut right into the wood.

Before Grams's illness, I always thought of myself as a happy, upbeat type of person. Bears used to tease that I was the original smiley face, the one responsible for the billons of yellow smiley faces endlessly circling the world. He wouldn't say that lately. Especially today. If anyone tried to make me smile, I'd bite their face.

"T?" calls Bears through the screen door. "Hey, T! I know you're in there. I saw you at the window."

I hear the creak of the stairs. Stupid creature. "Don't!" I shout.

"Don't what?" he calls from the middle of the staircase.

"You do not want to talk to me right now!" I yell.

"Yes, I do," he says, coming down the hall, totally unaware that Wolf Girl is going to snap his face off.

"No, you don't!" I yell as loud as I can.

I hear his breathing as he hesitates outside my room. Perhaps his animal instincts are kicking in and warning him of imminent danger. But the door of my room swings open, and he's in my lair.

He sees my eyes and freezes like an animal caught in bright lights. "What?" he says.

I narrow my eyes. "Why are you here?"

Bears doesn't answer right away. "You look like you're considering eating me for lunch," he says in a wary voice.

"You're too skinny. Why are you here?" I say again.

"I'm worried about you."

"Don't be."

"Too late."

And just the way he says it, kind of soft, soothes me like a warm day in winter. Then I cut to him kissing that nurse wannabe in the closet, and I'm stormy and cold again.

"T, it's the summer before our senior year, our last real summer," he says, staring at a Salt Rock poster I have on my wall. "Don't spend it in your room."

"Better here than in a supply closet in a stinking nursing home," I spit back.

"T . . ."

"I want to be alone," I say testily, watching the sun stream in my window and shimmer his hair.

"OK, OK," he says, backing out of my room, doing exactly what I've asked, exactly what I don't want him to do.

After he's gone I yank the Salt Rock poster off my wall. "You're history," I say, and I shove it under my bed.

22

THE NEXT DAY MR. MATHESON, Grams's friend from down the street, stops by. He used to be in and out of our place all the time. I knew Grams liked him, but for years I was scared of him. He has a scar down the right side of his face that pulls his mouth down so he looks like he's constantly scowling. On Halloween when I was in fourth grade, Peter Waxmell, a sixth grader who lived across the street from me, swore that Mr. Matheson had killed his former wife. "And he's going to get you next," threatened Peter.

It's funny to think of all that, looking at Mr. Matheson today. He's so old and looks so frail, it seems he'd fall over if I just tapped him on the shoulder. I've grown to like him fine because he's comfortable to be around.

"Good day, Taylor. May I please cut a few of the Cherish roses from the bushes along your front walkway?" he asks politely.

"Sure, Mr. Matheson," I say, amused that he knows the names of the roses.

He thanks me, giving me a quick bow, and hobbles off, little clipping shears sticking out of his back pocket.

As soon as I say goodbye, I hear a knock on the back door. I discover Mike on the porch, a toolbox hanging from his right hand.

"Hi," he says, as I step out onto the porch.

I notice that he's looking down at my feet. I bet he isn't staring at my feet so much as not daring to glance at my breasts.

"When do you go to Ebbie's grandmother's?" he asks my toes.

I relent. "I lied about that."

"Lied?" he asks, surprised.

"I don't know why," I mutter. "It just came out."

"Are you this strange with other people, or just with me?"

"I don't like the way I've seen you treat other people," I answer. "And I don't like the way you look at my body."

"OK, well, I guess I'll measure the porch," he says, backing away.

"Good idea," I say.

Mike presses his thumb on a red button, pulls out a long gold metal tape, and unrolls it along the porch railing. Absorbed by his task, he seems different from the Primate I know at school. Here, he's just a really cute guy, into a project.

"I don't know who you are," I say softly, surprising both of us with my words and my tone.

"What?" he says, looking disconcerted.

"I don't know what you think and stuff," I explain. "I've just assumed I know what kind of person you are, but I don't really know you."

I can't think of anything else to say, and it doesn't look like he's about to help. But then he surprises me by putting out his hand.

"Hi," he says, smiling widely. "My name's Mike Harkers. I'm here to fix your porch."

"Hi, I'm Taylor," I respond, feeling the pleasing warmth of his hand as we shake.

"Nice to meet you," he says. "Maybe we can hang out sometime."

"Maybe," I say, giving him an inviting smile that turns my maybe into yes.

"I'd better finish up here—I'm catching the Port Townsend ferry in an hour—but I'll be back tomorrow."

"If you need anything, let me know."

"Sure."

"OK," I say. "It was nice to meet you."

I wander back into the kitchen, smiling the whole way. I hear our mailbox squeak, so I head to the front door and find a postcard from Ebbie—a full-color photograph of a painter's palette. *Bet your fingers twitched when you saw this card! Love, Ebbie.* I smile at Ebbie's words but scowl at the photo. I wish this picture did make my fingers twitch, that I was holding a palette dripping with colors and a paintbrush poised over a piece I was as excited about as the painting I did in Zurich with James.

I carry the card out to the porch swing just as Bears comes walking up, holding a gigantic melon.

"Holy watermelon, Batman," I say.

"I'm lugging this thing over to the Peace Park for the potluck, and I thought you might want to go over together."

I've completely forgotten about the annual Welcome Summer party. Suki from the food committee called weeks ago to ask if we were bringing anything. I thought of Ebbie and said, "Yes, sandwiches."

"I'll be right back," I say. "Wait here!"

I have no idea what to do, since—other than leftover

fried rice from last night's takeout dinner and a few old bread ends at the bottom of the breadbox—there's virtually no food, not even peanut butter, in our house. I need Grams. She'd come up with something.

I realize that it's my turn to figure this kind of stuff out. Grams raised me to be independent and inventive; she taught me to take care of myself.

So, despite the lack of sandwich innards, I start concocting. Squashed marshmallows and raisins. Cocoa sprinkled on buttered bread ends. I open the fridge and drag out all the plastic containers. There are a couple of hard-boiled eggs rolling around in one of them, but they smell like pigs' toes. I find slices of dried-out pickles at the bottom of another container, and a third that has been taken over by long blobs covered in blue fuzz. Desperate for anything that doesn't stink and isn't covered in mold, I smash crumbled cookies into an applesauce jar and use that as a kind of chunky jam. I scratch leftover scrambled eggs from this morning's breakfast out of the frying pan, stir the scraps into some cottage cheese, and voilà, *fromage surprise.*

I cut the Sandwich Things into different shapes, slap them on a plate, and cover them in plastic wrap. If Ebbie saw this, she'd croak, but Grams would cheer bravo.

"Are you coming?" calls Bears.

"Ready!" I shout.

When I come out, Bears is looking at my postcard from Ebbie. "Did your fingers twitch?" he says.

"Stop reading my mail!"

"It was right here."

"So?" I say. "That doesn't give you permission to snoop."

"It was facing up, T. I didn't go rummaging through your drawers."

"I still don't like other people reading my mail. And no—my fingers didn't twitch."

23

NO ONE SAYS ANYTHING ABOUT my recycled sandwich wrecks. They probably just think I'm some sad kid who doesn't have a mother and doesn't know any better. That's OK with me.

At the end of the picnic, three of my sandwiches have bites out of them, one bite out of each sandwich, and I saw Chris Bayley feed her dog Kiva one. So far, no one has keeled over and died or even clutched their stomach in pain.

"Interesting sandwiches," says Bears as we beat a retreat from the park. "Looks like I missed a mess of fun waiting on your swing." He's trying to conceal a smile. "If I'd known you were in there smacking stuff at the counter and scraping up whatever stuck together, I'd have come on in and helped. Did you get all the mold off the butt ends of the bread before you slapped that crap on them?"

Even though I'm embarrassed, I'm happy to have Bears teasing me again. I'd forgotten how comfortable I am with him, how much fun it is to hang out together. "At least no one needed to have their stomach pumped," I say, and we laugh so hard we set the neighborhood dogs off barking.

"Taylor Rose, it's good to see you laughing," says Mr. Matheson, who's also walking home, carrying an empty plate under his arm.

"Hi, Mr. Matheson."

"How's that pretty grandma of yours doing today?"

Is he senile, that he doesn't even know Grams is dying?

"That woman is wild and sweet," he continues, oblivious to the spears I'm shooting at him with my eyes. "I'd give up beer for life to have one dance with that girl."

I want to tear off his lips. Smash his face in until he can't talk anymore. I can't believe I feel this monstrous. From laughing till the dogs howl to bashing in an old man's teeth. I'll get arrested for insanity or murder before I get over losing Grams.

"She's not doing well, sir," Bears cuts in. "She's down at the Golden Edges."

"I know that, son," says Mr. Matheson. "I've been to see her every morning since she got there. I happened to miss today because of getting ready for the picnic. So how does she seem to you?"

I glare at him so hard my head hurts. If he goes to visit her, why doesn't he see that she can't dance with him or anyone else now!

"Look here, Taylor girl. I know Alessa and I won't be

waltzing to *The Blue Danube* anymore, but that doesn't change the way I feel about her," says Mr. Matheson, softly but firmly. "I only have love for that grandma of yours."

I don't know what to say. The intensity of his feelings for Grams has drained out all my anger.

"Do you love raspberries the way your grandmother does?" he asks, as if we're starting the conversation all over again.

"Yes," I say quietly.

"Well, come by any day and gather a basket of them from my patch, as Alessa used to do. My raspberries need a female visitor every once in a while. Helps them grow sweet. Come by. And bring your boyfriend here." He winks at Bears and ambles off.

"Think you'll go through Murdering Matheson's gate to pick berries?" says Bears. "It might be a plot. Don't forget, you're his next scheduled victim!"

"I'd risk both our lives for those berries," I say.

Bears laughs. "It's nice to hear someone talk about Grams that way. What time is it?"

"Just after four."

"Got to go. See you!"

And he's gone. Probably meeting that candy-striped girl in some closet.

On the way home I can't stop thinking about what Mr. Matheson said. He talks about Grams like she's dancing in the kitchen, laughing and singing, even though he knows she just sits in a chair staring into air now. The way he spoke makes me feel confused. I'm happy to hear that he cares so much about Grams, but bringing her back to life like that makes me realize how much I miss her being Grams.

Dad comes in carrying a large bag of groceries under each arm. He stops and does a double-take when he sees the plastic containers sprawled all over the counter.

"Oh, no," he says. "Did I miss the neighborhood picnic?"

"Yes, including the commotion that the Jeffersons' Lab caused when he jumped up on the dessert table and sent cake and icing flying everywhere. On the bright side, you may have avoided a serious case of food poisoning."

"I'm sorry, Taylor. I wanted to go with you. I thought the picnic was tomorrow. I just bought nine bags of groceries at the Star store so we'd have bread and all the makings, as well as some *interesting food* in the house."

"Way to go, Dad! That would've been fun," I say. "But you didn't miss much—except the cakes and pies sliding onto the grass."

Dad manages a wimpy smile, but I can tell he feels bad.

"It's OK," I say, trying to let him off the hook. "I'd have missed it, too, if Bears hadn't staggered over with the biggest watermelon in the state of Washington."

"No, it's not OK," he insists. "I want us to do things, to spend more time together."

For the second time today, I'm speechless. *Whose dad is this?* I wonder.

"I've got to get the rest of the food," he says, plunking the two bags on the counter and heading back to the door.

"Want help?"

"No, I've got it," he says and pushes open the screen door. Then he pauses, turns, and grins at me. "On second thought, I'd love some help."

The trunk is packed with more food than I've seen in months. This might be the first time Dad's ever bought a week's supply of groceries at once. Usually he just grabs stuff we need the next day, like milk, O.J., or a carton of eggs. Carrying in groceries, something most people do every week of their lives, feels like an event at this house.

"Did you and Mom grocery-shop together?" I ask as we haul bags out of the car.

Dad looks puzzled, like I've asked him to solve a difficult math problem. "I suppose so. But I don't actually remember."

"What *did* you do together?" I ask.

"Laugh," he says. "We laughed a lot." Dad and I walk silently into the house, the bags crinkling as we thump them onto the counter. "Yes," he says, picking up the conversation. "Yes, we did grocery-shop together. She used to ride the back of the grocery cart like a scooter."

"She *did?*" I say, thrilled to imagine my mom shooting down the aisles at the Star store, probably laughing.

"Yes," he says, smiling. "I'd forgotten about that."

"She sounds nuts," I say happily.

"She was," he says, and laughs. "A free spirit."

I start putting away the cold stuff that needs to go into the refrigerator.

"I'd like to do more things together," says Dad again.

"Sure. We could ride grocery carts next time we're out of milk," I say, causing Dad to laugh again.

"Or play a couple of sets of tennis," he counters.

Since I was six, Dad has been trying—and failing—to get me enthusiastic about whacking a ball over a net. All I want right now is to keep him talking about Mom, to go through photo albums or old letters together—anything to bring her alive for me. But it feels so good to finally hear him talking like this that I don't want to wreck the moment by throwing in a no. "Tennis it is," I say, and I even manage a smile.

"Good," he says, tossing an apple from hand to hand. "I forgot to make it happen the last time we talked about it."

"That's OK."

We dodge around each other like kids playing tag as we stash the groceries in the pantry and fridge.

"I talked to Mr. Matheson today," I say, anxious to keep the conversation going.

"He's a good man," says Dad, discovering an empty cereal box and tossing it out. "A good friend to Grams, too."

"Yeah," I say.

Dad grabs a loaf of bread and motions me over to the breadbox as though he's the Seahawks' quarterback and I'm a wide receiver. I take a few steps and hold up my hands, and he throws a whole-wheat pass right into my arms.

"Did he know Mom?" I ask.

"I suppose he did," says Dad a little wistfully. "Of course he did. Was he at the picnic?"

"Yes," I answer as Dad leans down to stow a bag of potatoes in the cupboard. "Did Mom like picnics?"

He's down there arranging the potatoes for a long time. "She *loved* picnics," he says as he stands up and I can see that his eyes are red. "She loved summertime, walking by the ocean, being outside." There's a long pause where neither of us says anything. I hold my breath, hoping to learn more about what Mom loved.

"How's Bears?" asks Dad, clearing his throat. "Good friends are hard to find."

"Yup," I say, thinking how much I like having Bears back in my life. I used to be casual around him, kind of like he was a brother. But I don't feel so much like a sibling anymore.

"And how's your artwork coming along?" Dad says, catching me off-guard.

"I've told you already," I say, instantly defensive. "It's not. Why does everyone have to go on about that?"

Dad looks startled. "That's why I asked," he says. "You mentioned you were having a hard time, and I was wondering how you're doing." Then he truly surprises me. "I noticed your drawing pad was left outside and got warped, so I bought you a new one. It's out in the car."

I'm pleased and disgruntled at the same time, feeling that Dad's thoughtfulness is a challenge as well as a gift. "Thanks," I say, embarrassed about having yelled at him.

"You're welcome."

I want to hug him. I put down the box of granola I'm holding and kind of tip toward him. Just as I'm wondering whether to keep leaning in, Dad moves forward and gives me a quick, light hug.

"OK," I say, feeling both warm and awkward.

"Very OK," he says. "I'm going to make us some dinner."

"Make or heat up?" I say.

"I thought it'd be good to have something other than frozen food or takeout," he says with a wink. He walks over to his briefcase and pulls out a book, *Easy Recipes for New Cooks.* "Wish me luck!" he adds. "I'm going in."

"Luck!" I say. Stunned at this new development, I start walking out of the kitchen. Then I turn around. "Hey, do you want help?" I say, suddenly realizing it might be fun to spend more time like this with Dad.

"Sure," he says, and tosses me an onion.

24

THE NEXT DAY MIKE ARRIVES before I've even gotten out of bed. I hear his footsteps on the porch and then the *thonk* of a hammer hitting a nail. I curl up and read, trying to ignore him, but I can't concentrate, so I grab my sketchbook and start making lines. I remember summer mornings when I was little, curled in the sun on my bed, drawing thousands of pictures. I never paused to wonder what to draw. I sketched pictures as easily as I laughed.

I see Mike out in the garden, stretching in the sun, arching his back, and then rolling his shoulders. I watch him walk toward the house until he disappears under the porch roof. Now his absence is more distracting than his presence. The lace curtains brush my face as I lean out to listen to him working. When he stops hammering, I drift downstairs and slip out the screen door.

Mike's leaning against the porch, and he looks ready for a kiss. Oh . . . he has a nail between his teeth.

"Hi," he says, removing the nail. "Aren't you the girl I met here the other day?"

"Yes, I guess I am," I answer, feeling off balance, as if each word is a step on a high wire.

"May I have a glass of water, please?"

"Sure," I say, relieved to go inside for a moment. A few

days ago I'd have told him to use the hose at the side of the house, but I feel different now that we've moved to new terrain.

I fill up a glass slowly, drop in some ice to keep it cool for him, and take it outside. The ice cubes clink against the glass, ringing like little chimes, as I hold it out to Mike. He smiles when his fingers touch mine and then drains the water in one long swallow. While he drinks, I notice the shape of his hand and the line of his chin.

"May I have another, please?" he says, a drop of water lingering on his lips.

Our fingers touch this time, too. My body quivers and vibrates all the way down through the tops of my legs.

"Thanks," he says as I return with his second glass of water. "Porch is going well."

"Mmmm," I say, having difficulty finding words.

"I haven't seen anything on your easel out here since I started working. I thought you were, like, this artist person who painted all the time, not just at school."

My body stiffens and my teeth clench as I say, "I *am* an artist."

"Don't you use your easel?"

"I'm taking a break."

"A break? Do artists do that? I thought stuff comes into your brain and you, like, *have* to do it."

"When it comes, you do," I say. "And when it doesn't, you don't."

"Don't or can't?"

I feel dragon scales forming along my body and flames rising in my throat. If I replied, I'd scorch his skin.

"Well, what is it?" he says softly. "Can't or don't?"

"What's it to you?" I snarl.

"Hey, as someone you've personally painted, I know how into it you are," he says, giving me a dimpled smile. "So I'm curious."

Dragon Girl is vanquished as I realize he's a good sport about the day I smeared him. "I'm having kind of an artist's block," I say.

"Bummer," he says. "Last spring in baseball I went through a slump where I lost my edge and couldn't get my curve ball to break for two weeks."

I nod as a wedge of anguish settles in my throat. "I'm going to have breakfast now," I mutter, fleeing back into the kitchen.

After I down some juice and a slice of toast, I think about going to my room and trying to sketch again. But I find myself opening the screen door to see what Mike's doing instead. He's sawing a piece of wood. He's taken his shirt off; as he slides the blade back and forth, I see his shoulder flex and the muscles on his back ripple. His skin seems suddenly magnetic, as if my hand is being drawn to him and is about to snake out and touch him, slide up and down his tanned and glistening skin. Suddenly I want him to pull me in so I can feel the warmth of his skin on the soft insides of my arms.

I'm staring at his lats when a motorcycle zooms past. He turns to look and catches me gaping. "Are you looking at my body?" he says, grinning.

I laugh without meaning to and a blush colors my face. "I guess," I say.

"That makes us even," he says, sauntering over and standing close to me.

"I guess so," I say, reluctant to admit he's right. What is the difference between him gawking at me and me looking him over? "Although," I say, in a weak attempt to save face, "an artist looks at people differently. Like these muscles here." I trace his lats with an index finger. "I study the shapes of bodies."

"Me, too," he says, glancing at my breasts and smiling.

Another blush hits me in the forehead. This one must be fire red because heat radiates all over my body.

"Thanks again for the water," he says as he turns away and picks up the hammer. With his back to me, he starts hammering some nails deep into a horizontal board. His skin shines with sweat, his shoulders roll, and his back tenses with each swing. Everything Mindy used to say about the way he looks is right; he's gorgeous. The summer sun has already painted him brown, bronze, gold. All those days I hated him for staring at me, and now all I want to do is watch his skin ride his muscles. If he came over and kissed me, I'd wrap my arms around him and run my hands all over that golden skin.

25

I PUSH MY PENCIL INTO THE sharpener like I always do, as if life is just as it always was and drawing still something I do as naturally as brushing my teeth. I flip my sketchpad open and shoot my pencil across the page, attempting a rough sketch of Mike standing out in the garden. I place the tip of my pencil near the top of the page, envisioning the back of his shoulder blade, and stroke down, trying to capture the line of his V-shaped torso, right to the place where it dips in below his hipbone.

But even the memory of Mike's beautiful body doesn't make my lines flow.

I pretend I don't care, and I wander out to pick some lavender. As I arrange the fragrant flowers in a small vase on the porch, the early evening light casts soft shadows on Grams's perennial garden, bringing quiet thoughts of her.

When I was little and she'd tuck me in, she had a way of turning my bed to water. She'd sit on the edge, rolling me into her, and I'd be floating in a boat, sailing past the moon. It was magic and I loved having Grams tuck me in long past the time when I needed her to. Or maybe we always need tucking in, and it's one of the essentials thrown out by mistake. I remember I cried when I learned that Grams had given away my plastic plates, the ones with the dividers that kept all the food in different rooms, with designs of rabbits and Winnie-the-Pooh. I told her I needed my old juice cups for my stuffed animals—anything not to see them go. But being tucked in . . . well, that just stopped one night when I didn't even notice.

The feel of covers floating over my skin, followed by the weight of my comforter, always made my world seem just right. The tight feeling of being giftwrapped as Grams tucked in the covers—a safety measure to protect me from the Under-Beds, those creatures who slept below me and relished fingers and toes. And then the warmth as Grams leaned in and kissed me, her lips as soft as butterfly wings. When the door closed, and only the slice of light underneath it showed I wasn't alone, I'd sink into my mattress and start to dream before I even fell asleep.

I remember nights of crickets singing beside this old wooden porch and the creak of wicker as Grams settled into the rocker, leaning against the rose-flowered pillow on summer nights just like this one. She always had a cup of coffee in her hands, drops spilling and disappearing down cracks in the floor as she gestured while she talked. I'd breathe in the dark bean smell, willing her to begin a story from her life. I wanted to see her rest her cup on the porch floor and lean her head into the rose-patterned pillow, and hear, "Once, when I was about your age," or "I remember when your mom . . ." I'd will her eyes to slide off the porch, past the lilac bush, beyond the silver maple, and up into the starlit sky. I'd hope she'd forget that it was past my bedtime, as she often did once she had started one of her stories.

My hands would hold each other, hold my knees in place, hold my hope. When the streetlights flickered on, moths raced to touch faces with those glowing orbs of gold, and I'd freeze, hoping that Grams wouldn't notice the darkening sky. I'd hold my breath since a single noise, the click of a screen door, might bring Grams to her senses and send me to bed. I'd sit perfectly still, my body tensed, until I heard the magic words: "Once, when I . . ." Then she'd be off, the delicious telling would begin, and I'd sink into the sound of her voice.

A baby starts crying a few houses over, and I'm back, looking at the lavender and hearing the rustle of paper through the window as Dad turns the pages of his newspaper. When Grams was here, I was glad Dad stayed inside, because then I had Grams all to myself. Tonight I want to share stories with him.

"Dad?" I say so softly I doubt even the moths hear me.

He looks up, smiles, and then dips back to his reading. Did he actually hear me?

I try again. "Dad?"

This time he puts his paper down and comes over to the window.

"Do you want to come outside and talk?" I ask tentatively through the screen.

"Sure," he says. "I'll get some coffee and be right out. Want some?"

Since when do I drink coffee? But I'd love to smell its mysterious scent on the porch again. "Sure," I say.

Dad comes out balancing two mugs and a plate of cookies. I sink into the wicker rocker, leaning into the rose pillow, like Grams always did, while Dad takes the top step, where I used to sit. I hold the coffee on my lap feeling its warmth seep into me, breathing in the comforting smell.

"I used to love listening to you and Grams out here," Dad says.

"Listening to us?"

"I loved hearing Mamma tell stories." I've heard Dad call Grams "Mamma" all my life, so you'd think it'd pass over my mind like a sprinkler over my toes, but it always surprises me. "I'd sit in the chair closest to the window and pretend to read my paper so you wouldn't pay any attention to me."

"I never knew you listened."

"Didn't want you to," he says. "It was *your* time. But it was mine, too. I loved sitting inside, letting the sound of your voices drift through me. It was sweetly satisfying."

I start worrying about what I might have said that I wouldn't have wanted him to hear. "Did you hear everything?"

"Not the stuff you said about me," he says, and winks. "I was glad to hear every word; it was how I got to know you. Your mom would've known every inch of you. I don't know how to follow the maps to people, but Grams knows how. I learned about you by listening to the two of you talking." Dad takes a deep breath and lets it out slowly, as if he's doing some kind of yoga thing. "So, shall we tell a story?"

"One about Grams," I say, without any hesitation.

"Definitely," answers Dad, echoing my enthusiasm. "One of my favorites was the one about the time she went back to Canada to visit that old stone bridge she loved, back in her hometown."

"To wish Gow's Bridge a happy one hundredth birthday. Yes, I love that one," I say, feeling a smile slide across my face. I place my chin in my palm and my elbows on my knees and lean toward Dad.

Dad smiles, too. "Let's tell it together. We can help each other remember all the parts."

"You start," I say.

And he does.

After the story we sit quietly for a long time. It's dark now, and I can't really see Dad's face. I feel like I can say anything into the darkness.

"Dad, please tell me something about Mom—maybe something she liked to do, or what it was like to be with her."

I hold my breath. There's a long pause, with only the sound of crickets breaking the fragile silence on the porch.

"She was like a summer morning," he says softly.

This is so new, I don't know how to respond. I want to say something so brilliant that it surprises him into telling me more. But I don't. I just say, "Oh," and that "Oh" rings between us like the last bell from the church down the street.

I sit grinning in the dark, listening to crickets and watching the shadows of trees.

My mother was a summer morning.

26

THE NEXT DAY, AFTER LUNCH, I pass Mr. Matheson on my way into town.

"Good afternoon, Taylor."

"How are you, Mr. Matheson?"

"Fair to middling; can't complain. And yourself?" he says.

"OK."

"Where are you off to on this fine June day?"

I love the expressions he uses. "To Parker's art store for a paintbrush."

"That grandmother of yours sure is proud of your ability as an artist."

"Yeah. Grams used to say she couldn't make up her mind whose work she liked better, mine or Chagall's."

"Your grandmother certainly relishes the things she loves," he answers with a chuckle. "And I've enjoyed keeping up with your work over the years, myself."

"That's nice of you to say, although since Grams left, I haven't been able to finish a single piece of work."

"When you do get back up on that horse again, please consider me an interested party. I'd like to see whatever you come up with."

"Thanks, Mr. Matheson," I say, realizing what a truly sweet man he is. "I'd like that."

His eyes sparkle when he talks, and it seems like he almost always smiles. "So, that big show must be coming up."

"Yes," I say quickly, no longer interested in lingering if this is where the conversation's going. "Take care, Mr. Matheson."

I walk right through a perfectly chalked pink hopscotch design without making the effort to take a single hop. I don't really need a brush, but I want an excuse to be around paint and paper. Maybe if I hang in an art store, I'll be seized by inspiration and have to race home and paint an entire show.

While I'm browsing around Parker's, I spot a girl who looks familiar, but I can't figure out how I know her. I edge closer, trying to catch a full view of her face, and just as I'm about to walk over and say, "Don't I know you," I remember. Closet Girl! I quickly turn and scoot behind the large sketchpads, spying on her over the top of the tablets. I watch as the clerk tallies her order. She's picked out three brushes, a pad of paper, mat boards, and a dozen tubes of oil paint. Apparently, *she* doesn't have artist's block! I could hate this girl.

I'm concentrating so hard on her that I jump when I hear a familiar voice say my name. "Hey, T!"

"Ahh!" I gasp, so flustered to be caught like this that I can't say anything else. *If I don't speak, maybe I can make myself invisible,* whispers my inner six-year-old.

"Hey!" says Bears again, tapping me on the shoulder. "I hate to disillusion you, but I can see you."

"Hi," I say in a muffled voice, pulling my head from between the shelves.

"What are you up to?"

"Spying," I admit, because it's so obvious.

"On Evelyn?"

"Who's Evelyn?"

"The only other customer in the store," says Bears. "The person you're facing."

"Yes. Does Closet Girl paint as well as make out?"

"Evelyn. Yes, she paints."

"What, closets?"

And then we fall apart laughing, just like we used to do when we were kids. I grab on to Bears's shoulder to keep my balance.

"What's so funny?"

Evelyn has one hand on her hip. Her voice is sharp and demanding, like a detective at the scene of a crime. I feel as if I've just been caught shoplifting.

"Hi," I say, taking my hand off Bears.

"You look familiar," she says.

"I once gave you air when you were trapped."

"What?" she says quizzically.

"The closet at the Golden Edges," explains Bears.

"Oh!" she says, and blushes.

"This is Taylor, my oldest friend," says Bears.

"I'm not *that* old," I say, and Bears and I laugh again.

"Is this the girl who lives next door?" she asks Bears.

"That's me," I say.

Closet Girl runs her free hand through her long, straight hair and I notice that her hand has dried paint on it, just like mine often did. She tosses her head like a horse shaking off a fly, and her hair falls perfectly over her shoulder.

"Let's go, Barry," she says, standing between Bears and me and turning her back to me. "I want to finish that sketch of you."

"Give me a minute," he says, and walks around her to face me. "See ya, T," he says.

"Yeah," I say. "See ya, Bears."

Closet Girl looks annoyed and grabs his arm. I watch them walk out of the store together. Bears offers to carry her bag, but she shakes her head and holds it close to her chest. Bears glances over his shoulder and sees me watching. I wave.

I meander around for a while, feeling the textures of different brushes, flipping through sheets of paper—some pressed with flowers and grasses, some with silver threads. When I've had my fill, I head home and find Bears sitting on my porch.

"What are you doing here?" I ask.

"Waiting for you," he says.

"What happened to your modeling job with Closet Girl?"

"We had a bit of a fight," he says. "And I changed my mind about being her model."

He's sitting next to Grams's metal watering can, which is full. I suddenly feel playful. I swoop it up and drench him before he can scramble away. While I'm laughing, Bears pulls the can out of my hands and waters my hair through the holes in the spout. I grab on to the spout and we're face to face, yanking the can back and forth between us, riveted on each other's eyes. Then he jerks me toward him and I slip in the spilled water, falling into him, grabbing his shoulders to steady myself, drawing him into me, and we melt together. Our lips float toward each other, but Bears breaks away.

"OK, we can't do this," he says.

"I can do this easily," I say.

"Evelyn," he says, shrugging his shoulders. "I need to—"

"I thought you were merely her ex–male model," I interrupt, teasing him to regain my balance from the brink of the kiss. My body's a wild racing horse. I don't want to be having a conversation; I'm still shooting sparks.

"Let's just leave it here for now. I've got to get to work."

"OK," I say, but I'm not going to leave it here.

I'm going to carry the fire around all day.

27

THUNDER CRASHES AROUND the house all night long, including one large boomer that shakes my bed. As I'm dragging my comforter over my head, Dad pokes his head in to see if I'm OK. "I'm fine, Dad," I mumble, but I feel about three years old.

In the morning, I discover that the storm has strewn branches all over the garden and severed a huge limb from the silver maple tree.

As I make my way back to the porch, I spot a new paintbrush, clipped to the top of my easel with a note. *FOR WHEN YOU DO* is written in block letters on a sheet of oatmeal-colored paper, which has specks of crimson and pieces of rose petals embedded in it. I stand here looking out into the garden and twirling the brush. It's a beautiful sable brush, and I'm pleased by such a lovely gesture.

"What's up?" says Dad, joining me on the porch. "Can you believe what the yard looks like?"

"Nice paintbrush," I say, grinning at him.

"I saw it out here when I came down earlier to put the coffee on. Who's it from?"

If it wasn't Dad, it must be Mike or Bears. Mike asked me about painting just the other day, and he's been working out here on the porch, so it could be from him. Or Bears, making peace for not kissing me, or just because he's Bears.

"Maybe Mike. The guy you hired to fix our porch," I say.

"That's nice," says Dad. "He's the guy who's had a crush on you since you started high school, right?"

"How do you know about that?"

"I listened to you and Grams, remember? I seem to recall conversations about a jerk named Mike," says Dad, teasing me. "Is this the same Mike?"

"Yes."

"*There's* an elaborate plan to get a girl's attention," he says. "I wondered how he knew about this old porch needing help." He leans over and shakes the new part of the railing. "Not half bad."

"What do you mean, how he knew?" I say.

"He came by one day, pointed out the problems with the porch, and offered to fix it. Now I'm thinking it had more to do with seeing you than with making money."

I feel gold and sparkly like ginger ale in the sun and don't know what to say.

"It's quite the compliment, honey," says Dad. "This guy is probably doing all this work hoping you'll notice him. Other than being resourceful, what's he like?"

"I don't really know."

"Is he in your art class?"

"No! He is *so* not in my art class," I say. "He's a jock. He likes cheerleaders."

"I don't know about the cheerleaders, but he likes you, so he obviously has excellent taste in women."

While Dad goes over to check the silver maple, I stand twirling the paintbrush. Mike is doing all this work just to impress me! I can't help smiling.

"The silver maple doesn't look so good," Dad says as he's hosing off his hands. "I'll call Greg Vanman and have him check it out."

"What do you mean, check it out?"

"He mentioned a while back that it might be in trouble and have to come down."

"I love that tree, Dad."

"Me, too. But that doesn't mean it can't get sick. I'm off to work, sweetie, so I'll see you tonight. I have a new recipe I'm going to try out on us. I love you, Taylor." The screen door bangs as Dad vanishes inside.

"Wait!" I yell.

Dad sticks his head out. "Yes?"

"I love you, too, Dad. Bye!"

He comes out, his eyes bright, wraps an arm around my shoulders, and squeezes.

The sun's toasty on my face as I sit in a splash of sunlight, swiping the new brush back and forth as if I'm painting my palm. I close my eyes and concentrate on the soft sable bristles tickling my skin, painting my whole hand imaginary lavender. I feel a shadow sweep across the sun. When I open my eyes, Mike is standing beside me.

"Hi," I say, happy to see him.

"Feel good?" he says, nodding at the brush I'm still whisking across my palm. I turn the bristles around and paint a few soft strokes down his leg.

"When I'm finished here, do you want to go to the beach?" he asks.

I squint up at him, not sure what I want. "Maybe tomorrow," I finally say, dabbing a dot of invisible saffron on his knee.

"OK. You're welcome to stay out here and paint while I work," he says, gesturing at my new brush. "I'd like to see an artist at work."

"I'm not painting right now, remember? But thanks."

Mike raises his eyebrows, so I hold up the brush. He stares for a moment until I hold up the note. "Yeah," he says. "Right. Glad you like it."

"Thanks anyway," I say. So it *was* him! "Even though I'm not painting."

"I guess you can't know for sure when it'll come back for you—just like my curve ball. I mean, today could be the day you start painting again."

"Maybe," I say quickly. "But right now, I'm going into the kitchen to paint a blue bowl with white milk and some golden ovals of cereal."

While I'm preparing breakfast, Mike starts hammering nails into the flooring on the porch. I'm aware of him out there all morning—my body vibrates to the beat of each blow.

After supper, I'm snuggled on the porch swing, reading, when Bears saunters across the garden carrying a huge bunch of cleomes.

"Remember these?" he says, holding up the bouquet as he bounds up the steps.

Grams and I used to plant them every spring. We thought they looked like something from a Dr. Seuss book—punk flowers with crazy spiked hair and feathery seedpods sticking out all the way down their long leafy necks.

"Yes, I love those things!" I say, marking where I am in my book and placing it beside me. "Where did you find them?"

"Back of my garden," he says. "You planted them there."

"Are you out of your mind? I haven't been in your garden for eons!"

"You planted them the day after we escaped from seventh grade, the summer we planted them everywhere, remember?"

"Yes, of course," I answer, smiling at the memory of our plan to make cleomes the town's official flower. "But I haven't seen any since that summer, and anyway, they're not perennials."

"If you save their seeds after they've bloomed, you can plant them again every year."

"You've been collecting flower seeds for the last four years?"

"Yeah," he says. "Grams showed me how to do it."

He's surprising me every time I see him.

"If I saved a seed from the silver maple, could I grow another tree?" I say.

"Who knows? These are for you to take to Grams," he says, laying the pink flowers in my lap. "I thought she might remember them. And even if she doesn't, she loves flowers. Remember the summer she planted pansies in those purple high-heeled shoes?"

"Yeah," I say, smiling. I pick up the cleomes and turn the floppy flowers around in my hands. "Thanks," I say, standing up to go inside. "Are you sure you don't want to take them to her?"

Bears smiles and holds the back door open for me. "You do it," he says, and he's gone.

I'm smiling as I take a vase out of the cupboard and fill it with cool water.

Later I lift my self-portrait down from above the fireplace to take to Grams as well. Her room is bland, which the old Grams would never have allowed, and I haven't done a thing to help—except to rip down the owl. I unhook the moon mobile from above my bed for Grams, and I'll put Ebbie's cow udders above Grams's window, so she can hear the chimes whenever a breeze blows through her room.

28

THERE'S A NOTE ON THE COUNTER, Scotch-taped to the apple bowl. *Tennis, anyone? If yes, meet me at the courts at 1 P.M. I'm taking the afternoon off. Maybe we can see Grams, too. Love, Dad.*

I can't believe it. Even though I hate tennis, I love that Dad remembered. I grab an apple out of the bowl and toss it into the air.

I've got a few hours until I have to race around after a ball. I step out onto the porch and immediately smell Grams's fragrant Shakespeare roses—Fair Bianca, Wise Portia, and Othello, which grow white, carmine pink, and crimson. Grams crammed the house full of them when she was here. Anything that held water became a vase, and it didn't matter which room you went into, there were roses. Grams used to say she could put in an entire day just appreciating roses, so I take part of the morning to try it out. By the time I leave for tennis, the whole house smells like roses.

"Great!" says Dad when I swing open the gate to the court. He looks so pleased to see me that I grin.

"Hi, Dad. Since when do you take the afternoon off?"

"Since now," he says. "Since I've woken up and realized I'm missing out if I don't spend time with you."

"Oh, Dad!" It's terrific to have Dad say he loves me

like this. I feel more like dancing than like thwacking little yellow balls.

We play until my tennis racket droops and smacks against the court. I can't lift my arm above my knees, and the bottoms of my feet feel the searing heat rising from the scorching clay court through my sneakers.

"It's too hot," I call to Dad.

"Come on, Taylor girl. You can do it!"

"Ha!" I say back, and hold the ball instead of returning it to him. "Let's try a father-daughter activity that doesn't involve sweat."

"So you want another activity, do you?" says Dad, coming up to the net.

"Yeah. How about a boat trip to Alaska, so we can slide down some ice-cold glaciers?"

"How about some backyard badminton?" he says.

"Badminton's OK," I say, as we walk to a shaded bench. "Let's see—being on grass, way cool for blistering feet. Hearing grownups say 'birdie' like babies, that's humorous. Feathers flying above me, that's poetic. The soft *ping* of a rubber tip bouncing off of nylon strings, that's definitely musical. Yeah. OK, let's play badminton next time."

Dad laughs. "You're a poet," he says. "Me, I just love to whack the ball."

"I like hearing that sound, as long as it's in the distance and it doesn't involve me," I say.

Dad laughs again.

"Chasing a ball on hard, hot clay is just not my thing," I say.

"Your mom didn't like playing tennis either—that's what made me think of badminton. That was about the only competitive sport she'd agree to play with me."

"Cool," I say. This is the first time ever that he's volunteered anything about Mom. "What would she rather do than play sports?"

"She liked playing with the word *play.* I remember one weekend we were at the Gordons'. They'd just purchased a grand piano and they invited anyone who wanted to, to play. Your mom walked right over, sat down, and kind of went crazy at the keyboard, even though she had no idea what she was doing. 'Hey, Max,' she shouted across the room to me, 'I'm playing with the piano!'

"Another time, when your mom was invited to play bridge, she pulled a chair right up to the table and arranged her hand of cards like she knew the game. But she didn't. She put down whatever card she felt like and drove everyone crazy." Dad's smiling and bouncing a tennis ball on his racket as he talks.

"Grams never told me these stories," I say.

"I guess because they're mine to tell," he answers. He looks off over the trees. "I haven't really taken time to play for a while."

"You did today."

"I did something even more important," he says. "I

played with you." And he salutes me with his racket. "What else do you like to do?"

"I like meditative stuff, going inside myself, shading in lines on a white page. And I like listening to the outside world, too, like the sound my pencil makes when I draw broad strokes, and the whisper of a sable brush sliding across a canvas. That's my kind of playing."

Dad's listening so closely to me that it makes me want to keep coming up with things to tell him.

"I'm thinking more of the good stuff about Grams," I say, bouncing my racket against my sneaker. "For a while I couldn't think of anything except how scared I was and how weird she is now."

Dad catches the ball as it bounces up off his racket and tosses it to me. "I miss her," he says. "And I'm learning how vital it is to picture her telling stories, or dancing, or wrapping her arms around someone in a huge hug, instead of seeing her only as my mother who has grown old and only sits and stares."

"Yeah," I say. "Around Grams, life felt like recess."

Dad looks up at me quickly with such a huge grin that I start to laugh. "Life with her *was* like recess," he says, nodding his head. "And I had a similar feeling the other night, when we told each other one of her stories. I liked sharing something with you."

"Me, too," I say, leaning over and giving Dad's elbow a squeeze. "Sharing Chinese takeout just doesn't do it for me. I need stuff that's more filling, like stories."

As I look at Dad, I feel light seep into me the way morning slowly arrives. I've been angry with him for being different from Grams. I've blocked him out because he isn't wild and outspoken. I don't want to do that anymore.

"Let's shower and go see Grams," says Dad, rumpling my hair.

"I'd like that," I say, smoothing my hair down. And, for the first time since Grams got ill, I really do want to see her.

After we change, I grab Bears's grand bouquet of cleomes. Dad carries the bag with my artwork and the mobile and chimes.

"I love what you said about Mom being like a summer morning. Does that mean she was warm and sunny?" I say, as we walk along toward the Golden Edges.

Dad stops walking and stands still. "Yes, it does," he says, nodding and smiling. "Your mom was sun and blue sky."

"That's beautiful."

"So was she."

It feels good to go through the doors with Dad, and we walk side by side down the hall to Grams's room, chatting. She beams as we come through the doorway and shows us her hands as if she's just discovered them. Dad takes one from its flight in the air around her and holds it. He looks at her as if he's her parent, lovingly taking his child's outstretched hand. I come up beside Dad, take Grams's other hand in mine, and hold out the flowers in front of her eyes.

While Dad arranges the cleomes in a vase, I open the bag and start taking out my artwork. I show Grams each piece before finding a place for it. I haven't asked permission from the staff, a lesson I learned from Grams. "Better to ask forgiveness than permission, sweetheart, as long as you're not hurting anyone," she'd say. I stand on a chair and hang the chimes over the window. When I flick them and make them sing to Grams, she smiles.

Just as I push a tack into the ceiling to dangle the moon above Grams's bed, a nurse sweeps into the room to ask if Grams wants juice. She frowns to see me up on the bed, but then she spots the mobile.

"Oh, Mrs. Wickham," she says, turning to Grams. "This is lovely. You have the moon to keep you company while you sleep."

As she helps me down, I see her nametag. "Thanks, Susie," I say.

She winks and backs out of the room, saying, "I don't need to know what's going on in here right now."

"If we need any special favors, we'll have to remember to ask Susie," Dad says.

We put my fourth-grade self-portrait above Grams's headboard, and I smile to see the plums hanging from my turquoise hair. When we're finished, Grams's room looks more like someone's living room than a waiting room.

On the way home, as we're passing the Star store, Dad says, "Let's make lemonade."

He keeps surprising me. In biology class, Ms. Weidner told us that our skin doesn't stay the same; our cells are new every day—outside and inside—so we shouldn't get so stuck on how we think we are, how solid and permanently in place we think everything is. Change is a part of everything, even our skin. And at the same time, even though Grams has changed, everything I love about her is still true.

Dad and I choose strange-shaped lemons and ones with dashes of green, because that's what Grams always did. It turns out neither of us knows why, but it's a tradition now. I wonder how many other family traditions make no sense. We put our weird lemons into two bags and carry them home in silence. As we walk along, I think about Dad losing his own recess mom and my blue-sky mom. He's had to say goodbye to two of the most special people in his life. I switch my lemons to the outside and tuck my hand in his arm. He leans into me and smiles as we walk home together.

"TAYLOR!" DAD CALLS.

I'm sitting on the porch swing, so deep into a biography of Georgia O'Keeffe, the Santa Fe artist, that when

Dad shouts my name, I'm so startled I drop the book.

"Out here!" I yell back, leaning down to scoop it up and examine the pages for damage.

"I just heard from Greg Vanman, the tree guy," Dad says, coming out the door. "We have to take the silver maple down. The huge branch that fell is an indicator that the tree's rotting. It's too dangerous to leave it up."

"No!" This tree grew alongside me. I measure the seasons by its buds, baby leaves, full green, and reds in autumn. "I think of it as *my* tree," I say to Dad.

"I didn't realize it meant so much to you," he says, walking toward the door.

I can't concentrate to read anymore. I wander out into the garden and lean against the silver maple, pushing my cheek into the trunk and letting the bark etch designs into my skin.

I call Bears and make a plan to get out of here tomorrow before the tree guy comes. But the chain saw wakes me the next morning, and the light in my room changes as a branch crashes past my window. I bolt out of bed, throw on clothes, and race for my bike.

When I knock on his door, Bears comes out pulling on a T-shirt and carrying his backpack. I leap on my bike and pump my legs so hard I leave the earth and eat the wind. I shoot off the end of our street, over the park, and on out to the ocean. I push my thighs until it feels as though they'll burst into flames, and I ride right onto the beach. I bound off my bike while the wheels are still spinning, letting it fall onto the sand as I keep running until I collapse on the edge of the shore.

Eventually, Bears flops down beside me, laughing. "You're completely nuts," he says as we lie panting, trying to catch our breath. "Want an orange?"

"I couldn't peel it," I say limply.

"Here." A ribbon of orange spirals down to the sand. Above it a peeled orange sits cupped in his hand. He pulls it apart, spraying us both with a warm mist and the scent of orange, and places half of the moist fruit in my palm.

"Thanks," I say. "For the orange. And for being there for me."

"You're welcome. I'd hate to watch that tree crash down."

We sit in silence, peeling off orange sections and listening to the waves rolling small pebbles and shells onto the shore. When we've finished eating, Bears starts digging a hole. I join in, scooping handful after handful of sand, feeling the sand turn from light and warm to cool and heavy as we dig deeper.

"I took the bouquet of cleomes to Grams. I'm sorry I gave you grief about visiting her," I say after a while.

I wiggle my toes in the sand as we dig. When the hole gets large enough, I put my feet in, and so does Bears. We start covering our legs with sand, and he wiggles his toes over so they touch mine.

"Thanks for coming back into my life, Bears. I can't believe we almost lost each other." I can feel his toes warm on top of mine now, like our feet are making out in the wet sand.

"Hey, if we'd really lost each other, I'd have plastered photos of your face all over the post office bulletin board under 'Missing Persons' until I found you. This was a hell of a lot easier. Want a bagel?" he says, brushing off his hands and rummaging in his backpack.

I take a bagel out of his hand and lean into him. "Dad says that taking down the maple will allow more sunlight into the garden, so now we'll be able to grow raspberries."

"Grams always said it was a shame that old tree had been planted where it was, because it would have been the perfect spot for a berry patch," says Bears. "Remember?"

"You know that old poster in the library that says, 'When life hands you lemons, make lemonade'? I say, 'When a tree falls, plant raspberries.'"

I sit munching and looking around. Offshore a cormorant dives below the waves and surfaces with a shimmering fish. A tern lands out on the rocky point. I squint at the rocks around it, taking them out of focus until they become just masses, lights and darks, abstract forms.

"What are you doing?" asks Bears.

"Squinting. I'm playing with shapes and light."

"Play with me instead," he says, pulling his feet out of the sand and dragging me up.

We race along the shoreline, scattering seagulls, splashing each other, and sometimes holding hands.

30

I NEVER KNEW COOKING could be so loud. When I hear the pots start clanging like Chinese gongs, I know that Dad has started dinner. The sound effects eventually increase in intensity until it sounds like a Tom and Jerry cartoon, with frantic slamming of closets and drawers and the echoing din of pots and saucepans being banged together.

"Anyone hurt in here?" I ask, coming cautiously into the kitchen.

"I'm right as rain," Dad says, grinning over a steaming pan of sauce. "Here, sample this and see if your taste buds don't beg for more."

"I could drink a mug of it," I say, and Dad smiles happily.

I offer to stir the various pans while Dad checks the recipe. Grams was so relaxed about cooking, I never realized there were so many things you had to know to do it right.

"Quick, plates!" Dad shouts.

I race around grabbing plates and forks, pouring milk, buttering bread, and helping Dad carry everything out to the porch. We relish our pasta with Dad's sauce (made of three different cheeses, he proudly announces) and chunks of sautéed vegetables. I watch a squirrel sitting exactly where the silver maple used to be and, I imagine, looking over at us accusingly. There's still sawdust on the grass. I miss the way the tree's branches divided the sky, breaking up all that blue with dark lines and clusters of green. But once we get some raspberry bushes planted, maybe Dad will learn how to make jam and pie.

"Delicious meal—thanks again, Dad," I say.

"Not bad for baked rats." He winks at me. "So, Taylor," he says more seriously.

"Yes, O King," I reply. I used to say "O King, live forever!" whenever he pleased me. I haven't called him "O King" in a long time.

"I've been thinking. How would you like to move into Grams's room? It's larger than yours and you've always loved it."

I feel like a kid being toppled by an unexpected wave at the beach. "No!" I say more forcefully than I mean to. "I loved it because she was in it."

"It's just something to think about," he says, looking surprised. He must have thought I'd be pleased.

"I don't want to," I say. "Don't change anything."

We sit in silence for a while. I can hear guitar chords floating out of Bears's open bedroom window, and the sound settles me down.

I do love Grams's room, the way it smells, the way it reminds me of her. I sometimes go in there to sit and think. But actually moving in would make it seem as if I've shoveled Grams into the past, almost as if she's already dead.

After we clean up, I step into her room. I like that the dresses in her closet are all lined up, waiting, that the smell of her powders and perfumes mingles with her clothes. I delight in opening her drawers and seeing her brooches and scarves, touching the soft silks. Her hairbrush is old-fashioned looking, the bristles soft and worn. It belonged to her mother—my great-grandmother—and when Grams brushed my hair with it, she often told me stories about her mother, Barbara Maxwell Price. Wisps of gray hair are sticking out the sides. I pull the brush slowly through my own mop of hair, remembering when I was younger and I'd sit on the little plum ottoman in front of Grams as she brushed my hair till it shone.

"Hi there," Dad says. I spin around feeling guilty, like someone caught trespassing.

"Why don't you just clear out a few drawers for yourself?" he asks. "You could even move some of your winter clothes in here and free up space in your room." He leaves without waiting for a response.

"Whatever," I say to the doorframe, but I realize that I actually like the idea. Maybe I could turn Grams's room into my studio. I've always wanted my own space for painting, and Grams would love that I was using her room for creating art.

I wander back to my room carrying Grams's brush, pull it through my hair once more, then place it on the nightstand beside my bed. Glancing out the window, I spy two people leaning against the oak between Bears's house and ours. They're standing so close, they might as well be in a closet. The guy, it must be Bears, has both his arms around the girl, and she has her arms all wrapped around him. My stomach crunches into a hard ball, but I can't stop watching. The guy could be Neil from two houses down—it's hard to tell. I push off from the windowsill like a swimmer off the end of a pool and walk back to Grams's room. I pick up a perfume bottle, remove the top, and wave it back and forth under my nose, closing my eyes and remembering a time when Grams was here.

I open and close drawers, looking for one I can empty and feel OK about using, sharing with her. The scarf and belt drawer is already half empty. As I lift a handful of scarves, I feel something hard, untangle it, and find a notebook. When I thumb through the pages, I discover Grams's handwriting, and my heart twangs.

The first entry I read is dated just a few weeks before I found her in the kitchen. It says, *My body feels strange. It's not the regular getting-old feeling. Something's not right. I'm fading in and out, like a candle flickering in a breeze. Sometimes I'm afraid I might be blown right out.*

I'm stunned by her words, by knowing she felt like a candle about to be snuffed out. I feel a little dizzy reading this and wonder if I should be looking at it without Grams's permission. She always encouraged me to share my thoughts, which is what made us so close. I'm not sure what she'd want, but I can't stop turning the pages. It's like hearing her voice, the way it used to sound.

There's a grocery list with weird-sounding food on one page. I'll use it to go shopping. There are quotes copied from books. And then a poem.

ME

I drift, lift away.
My body waits,
unsure.

Deep in my weakening bones my body knows
I won't be true, won't always come home.
One night I'll lose my way,
falter in my flight,
turn to light.

Once light,
these bones will crash
beneath my flight.

Grams crashed, just like her poem says. I can't imagine holding such a scary feeling—making toast, say, something so everyday, and at the same time knowing her body was sliding away from her. Hugging me good night and feeling herself fading like twilight.

These pages bring Grams back into the house. I haven't heard her real voice in so long, and now here it is, her voice in my hands. I've always known Grams had notebooks lying around. She was often curled up on the stuffed chair in her room, writing. I'm so used to it, I didn't think about it. How could I not have wondered about what she wrote?

I take the notebook back to my room and sit cross-legged on my bed, immersed in the entries. This is even better than breathing in the smell of her dresses or perfume. Better than the picture on my dresser of the two of us laughing.

(Taylor, Christmas morning when she was three.)

GIFT-WRAPPED

Christmas morning,
holding the first present.
She lifts her arms to stars, sky,
top of tall pine.
Shouts,
"Let it out!"

She used to recite this poem every Christmas morning. I can read it with my eyes shut. I turn the page to read one last entry, and an envelope falls into my lap. On the front is written *For Taylor Rose, after I'm gone and it's time to let go.* My heart flutters like a hummingbird's wings. I slip the letter into my top dresser drawer and fall asleep holding Grams's book in my arms.

31

I DREAM OF WALKING INTO OZ, following the Yellow Brick Road into the heart of the wizard's kingdom, and demanding what I want. Pounding on some great door, pestering the guard until I'm allowed in, and then finding my way straight to the wishing chambers. Here is what I want—a heart, a brain, courage, home. I want it all, and I want shoes that gleam and friends by my side. And *poof,* all I need do is click my heels, just click, and every single one of my dreams comes true. That's all, and I'll wake up right where I belong.

Instead, I wake up on June 25, the last day for mailing portfolios to Salt Rock. I'm disappointed and embarrassed. I brush my teeth like it's any other morning, choose earrings like I usually do—determined not to make a big deal out of the fact that I didn't get it together, that I let this chance vanish. I wish I'd figured out how to break through and get the work done, as a tribute to Grams and as a message to myself that I can step up to make my dreams come true. But I'm no Dorothy.

I head out the back door, grab my bike, and ride to Walkerton's Variety Store. I'll buy a new journal and follow my thoughts that way. Become a writer instead of a painter. Grams used plain old notebooks, nothing special. I'll get the same kind, so I won't feel like my thoughts have to be perfect, or even poetic. A journal with lines, because I'm not going to draw anymore.

I select a beige spiral notebook as ordinary as I feel, but then I see a row of fancy journals. There's one with mint green swirls and mauve stars that I can't resist. After trying out all the pens in the store to see which one glides best across the paper, I go for a turquoise pen that has a smooth, fine point and the design of a dragon breathing fire along the barrel, and head home.

Mike's working on the porch, so I carry the old red-and-white-checked picnic blanket out to the far garden and stretch out in the sun to write. Because Grams is the one who has given me the idea to do this, I start by addressing her.

I'm starting a journal just like you. I was going to get an ordinary steno pad like yours but I saw a design I loved and couldn't resist it. I'll still slap my ideas down in here, even if it is fancier than I feel. I found the envelope in your journal. I guess that means you knew I'd read it and that it's OK, because I am. I'm reading every word. I'm starting to understand what you were thinking and feeling, now that you can't talk to me. Thanks for the envelope. I put it in a safe place.

This is hard for me to tell you, even though I know you'll never read it, but I can't paint anymore. I got into Salt Rock, just like you knew I would, and I blew it. I didn't send in a single painting and the deadline is today. Something about missing you has crowded out my ability to paint. I've decided to try writing. What I want to say to you is, Please stop fading! Don't leave me alone! I need you. What the hell am I supposed to do without you around to iron me out when I get wrinkled?

I rave on and on like this for pages. Then I start in on Bears. *What's with Closet Girl? Are you two together or not? I wonder how he kisses.* Next, I write about Mike. *Nice lips. I bet he's a good kisser. How would Bears feel if he saw me kissing Mike?*

When I finish, I fall back on the lawn, feeling the soft grass touching my palms, and imagine the whole round planet turning me slowly around in space. I feel exhilarated to have washed all those words out of my body. Perhaps that leaves room for something new.

When I get to the porch, Mike is just packing up his toolbox. "What's up?" he says.

"Nothing much," I answer. "How about you?"

"I just finished the job," he says, running his hand up and down the handle of the hammer he's holding. "Now you can ram into the railing and you won't go crashing into the garden."

"Well, that's a load off my mind," I tease.

"Do you want to go to the beach?"

"No," I say automatically. Bears is lifeguarding there, and I do not want to be in the same place as Bears and Mike.

"How about walking up to Courtney's Woods?" he says.

"That'd be fun," I say. "I haven't been there in a long time." I'm listening to my voice have this conversation, almost as if I'm eavesdropping on myself.

"Can I use your bathroom to wash up?" he asks, picking up his backpack and slinging it over his shoulder.

"Sure," I say. "Go straight through the kitchen and take your first left."

I sit on the porch steps and start writing again. *Being with Bears makes me want more. I don't know why I don't just grab him and kiss the living daylights out of him. Mike holds his lips like the beginning of a kiss when he hammers.*

I'm still writing when Mike comes back out. "Man, I'm roasting," he says.

"You just washed up," I say, turning to look at him.

"Suddenly, I'm hot again," he says, raising his eyebrows at me.

Oh, yeah, he's hot—standing here in a black cutaway muscle shirt, droplets of water glistening down his neck to his bare belly. "I could spray you down with the garden hose."

"Would you dry me off afterward?"

"All over," I say. I can't believe I'm flirting with this guy.

"Yeah?" he says.

"Maybe," I answer. I don't know if I really mean what I'm saying, but I lead him onto the lawn, casually open up the faucet, and when the hose grows firm, direct a full blast up and down his body.

"No!" I shout, laughing, as he yanks the hose away, spraying me until I'm soaked all the way through and dripping on the grass.

Mike is staring at my breasts under my wet T-shirt. I'd normally cross my arms over my chest and turn away, but I don't. Instead of feeling shy, I feel defiant and jazzed.

"Yes, I have breasts," I say. "What of it?"

Mike blinks, but he doesn't look away.

32

AS WE SIT SIDE BY SIDE IN THE SUN drying off, Mike picks up my hand. "Want me to read your palm?" he says.

"Don't you need a turban and incense?" I tease.

"I don't need any extra accessories." He switches over into a deep and mysterious voice. "You will meet a handsome guy who will take you into dark woods."

"Does he look like a wolf, and is he wearing my grandmother's nightgown?" I ask.

Mike wiggles his eyebrows up and down in a mock sinister way.

"In most versions the wolf gets killed," I say in a wicked voice.

"Wait, there's more," he says, peering down into my palm. "The wolf will live happily ever after."

"What an intriguing twist you've spun on the ending," I say.

"The better to lure you into the woods, my dear," says Mike. He stands up and holds out a hand to me. "Let's go do it."

"To the woods," I say, grabbing his hand and feeling his soft, warm palm against mine.

He pulls me in close to him, the backs of his fingers brushing against my breast, before he lets go of my hand. "Grab your sketchbook," he says, gesturing to my easel. "I'll carry it for you."

"What's up?" I ask.

"I have an idea. And that's all you're going to get out of me right now," he says with a smile.

Those dimples of his are like fireworks, flashing inside of me. I hand him the sketchpad, pick up a pencil, and follow him toward the woods. As we walk along side by side, I lean into him ever so slowly, feeling the gold hair on his arm tickle my skin like butterfly kisses. Bare arms are all I think about as we walk uphill, and then, without planning to, I reach out and touch the soft part of the skin on the inside of his bicep.

"You have strong arms," I blurt out.

I didn't mean to say that, and I can't believe I touched him. I bend down and pick a buttercup to mask my embarrassment.

"For someone who doesn't like me noticing her body, you sure notice mine," he says.

"I practice hypocrisy."

"You're good at it," he says, and then he changes the subject. "Can I check out your sketchbook?"

"If staring at blank pages is your idea of a good time, knock yourself out."

"Excellent!" he says, showing his teeth. "The better to pose for you, my dear."

"*What?*" I say.

"That's my idea," he says. "I'm offering to pose."

"And which position were you going to suggest, Mr. Wolf?" I ask, poking him in the stomach.

We're hitting words back and forth like tennis balls, a thin net between us.

"How do models usually pose?" he asks.

"Nude," I say, wanting to catch him off-guard.

"At *school?*" he says incredulously, looking like he might be ready to give up baseball for sketching.

"But we're not in school now," I say with a smile. "Still offering?" *What am I saying!* My body's moving faster than my brain.

"Oh, yeah," he says. *"Definitely."*

I walk silently beside him, but inside my head a voice is chanting, *What am I doing, and where is this heading?*

"I could pose for you when we get to Courtney's Woods," he says. "I know a quiet spot where no one else goes."

There's thunder rolling around his words, but I keep

moving toward the danger. "Really?" I say, while tigers race under my skin. "Do you often pose nude there?"

He just raises his eyebrows and smiles in a *Wouldn't you like to know?* kind of way.

What the hell, I think, *why not?* I'm not six years old. I'll just draw him. Or try to. That's what artists do.

"OK," I tell him, "You're hired."

"Really?" he says, stopping next to me. "You're really up for this?"

"Yes," I say, staring directly at him. "Are you?"

"Absolutely," says Mike, grabbing my hand and moving us full steam into Courtney's Woods.

"Where do you want me to pose?" asks Mike, when we get to the spot he's led us to.

"How about over there, in front of that log," I say, pointing to the trunk of a fallen hemlock.

I act busy sharpening my pencil on a rock. I've never seen a guy nude before, and the reality of what's happening makes me feel like Gretel just before she breaks off the first bite of candy from the witch's hut. Out of the corner of my eye, I see Mike face away from me, grab his shirt, and pull it over his head. His back is sleek and tanned. I run my eyes along his shoulder blades and the shape of his muscles, wishing I could force myself to walk over and touch him. When he starts to unzip his jeans, though, I focus on my pencil and keep sharpening. If he doesn't hurry up, the pencil's going to be ground down to a nub.

When he asks me how I want him to pose, my brain vanishes.

I have no idea. I have no idea. I have no idea.

"Standing," I say, fumbling my sketchpad open. "Or sitting. Or lying down."

"Choose one," he says.

I'm trying to think of a pose where I won't have to see him full frontal. "With your back to me," I finally blurt out.

Relief sweeps through Courtney's Woods.

"No problem," he says.

I stare at his buns, which are as brown as his back. *He must sunbathe nude,* I think while I look at the blank page and try to concentrate on my approach to the sketch.

"How long will this take?" he asks.

"As long as it takes," I say.

"Are you staring at my butt?"

"Yes," I say. "I have to start somewhere."

I place the point of my pencil on the paper, and a small line appears. Then the pencil starts to move, pulling my hand along with it. Lines begin to form, following the long muscles down either side of his spine that form a wedge, a V, right above his rear end.

The sketch is going so well and so quickly that I begin to feel a long-lost spark re-ignite within me. Or maybe I'm feeling something else, like heat from Mike's body. In that moment of self-awareness, I grow confused and draw lines I don't want.

"I'm finished," I say, frustrated and suddenly flustered and self-conscious about being in the woods with a naked boy. I'm in way over my head. I don't need my *palms* read, I need my *head* read!

"Can I see?" he calls over.

"Get dressed," I say, looking at my sketch and not at him.

I hear the sound of Mike pulling on jeans and then the crunch of leaves and twigs as he comes alongside me. He leans over my shoulder and I feel his breath on my neck.

"Models aren't allowed to get this close to the artist," I say, trying to be light and funny.

"No?" he says.

"No."

"I guess you're lucky then," he says.

"Am I?" I say, feeling my palms getting moist.

"Oh, yeah," he says. "Come here, beautiful creature!"

My heart is pounding all over my body. He slides in front of me and pulls us together. His hands are hot on my waist, and as if in slow motion I see his lips moving toward mine. Before our mouths touch, I shift my head and his lips only brush my cheek. He pulls me in hard. But I pull back. I want to kiss him. *Someone.* He leans in again, but I swing my head away.

I really thought I wanted that kiss, felt my body quiver, even urged it on. I wanted to feel the pressure of arms around me, kisses pouring warmth through my body. But

I don't think it's Mike I want. Not this kind of kiss. I want sweet kisses from someone who knows me and loves me.

"What the hell is wrong with you?" he says in a growly voice.

I wish I could say something that makes sense, but I can't find the words.

"Don't tell me I got the signals wrong," he persists. "You've been coming on to me all week."

"Is that what you think?" I ask, stalling for time.

"Oh, please!"

"Well, so have you," I say lamely.

"Yeah, but I followed through. You knew this was where we were heading."

"Maybe this is the part of the story where Little Red Riding Hood sees the big, bad wolf for who he is, and runs."

"You saw the fur and the big teeth before we got in here."

"It was about art," I say, knowing how stupid this sounds.

"Oh, yeah, right," he says. "Like you'd go into the woods with any guy and let him get naked in front of you. Tell me that wasn't a come-on!"

"It was art," I say again, my voice growing fainter.

"Give me a break," he says. "You haven't sketched in months."

I shift from foot to foot, beginning to feel trapped, like a small animal in a tight cage.

"Come here," he says, moving behind me, lifting my hair, and kissing the back of my neck.

Oh, this feels good. I sigh as the pleasure of his lips on my skin takes my breath away. As his lips slide down and across my shoulder, I relax into his kisses. He nibbles his way back up my neck to my ear. When he licks around the lobe of my ear, I hear his breath, like a soft breeze. My eyes close and I'm mist. Fog. I just want to continue feeling like this and not think about anything else. He pulls me down beside him onto the soft pine needles, and the sketchbook falls to the forest floor. I feel soft and melty, like cotton candy. Then he begins to slide his hand up my shirt.

"No," I say softly.

But his hand doesn't stop. He rolls over on top of me. I push, but I can't get out of his grip. He ignores me and kisses my neck, taking tiny licks behind my ears as he pulls me closer into him.

"*No!*" I say louder, trying to squirm out from under him. He's smashing his whole weight into me. I feel cold and scared, and I can't move. I'm beginning to think maybe this is my own fault, that I deserve this. I did lead him on. I did come here. But just as I'm starting to think about giving in and giving up, I stop myself. Yes, I got myself into this. But I don't have to go one step further. I can save myself.

"No!" I shout, shoving him fast and sharp. My arms push against him with a jerk. My legs shoot me off the forest floor with a force that startles him, and he loses his grip on me.

"Get over yourself," he says, trying to grab me again. "You know you want it."

I back away from him. "Not like this," I say. "Not with you."

I scoop up my sketchbook and take off running, leaving my little nub of a pencil behind.

33

I DIDN'T GET A PAIR OF GLITTERY shoes out of the deal, but I had my own moment as Dorothy. My heart and courage finally saved me, and my own two feet got me home—without a single click of my heels.

I made it out of the woods with a partial sketch, a small blemish in a sketchbook. So I rip that boy right out of there, clearing the way for sketches I care about. I stand on the sidewalk outside my house, tearing Mike's body into fragments and tossing them into the wind. A few catch in a gust and blow up and into the rosebushes. The rest scatter down the street.

I follow their flight and see Halle, the little girl from three houses down, racing after them like a kitten after butterflies. She chases pieces of my sketch around the sidewalk and almost out onto the street. She sees a few in the bushes and collects them like she's picking berries. I watch as if she's a movie.

"Here," she says, walking over to me and holding out the scraps. "How come you ripped up your picture?"

"I don't like it," I say, tears starting to trickle down my cheeks.

"Did you hurt yourself?" she asks.

"Almost," I say.

"Are you OK?"

"Pretty much."

"I can draw, too," she says, her voice filled with conviction.

I smile back, and she perks up like a puppy that's been patted on the head. "Want to see?" she says, holding up a purple crayon.

I nod and bend down, opening my sketchbook and placing it on the sidewalk. There are bits of purple crayon showing underneath her fingernails. She crouches over the paper and starts drawing right away. No waiting for ideas, no pausing to think, she just draws. Out it comes—lines all over the page making some kind of wild and happy picture.

"That's great," I say when she looks up at me.

"I know," she says happily, holding out her crayon to me. "Do you want to draw something?"

"I can't right now," I say. "I've forgotten how."

She looks puzzled. "How can you forget how to draw?"

"I don't know."

"You'll remember," she says with a smile, trying to cheer me up. "Sometimes I forget my phone number, but then when I forget to think about it, I remember."

I smile at her bright face. "Same for me," I say. "I'm glad you reminded me about that."

"Can I come draw with you when you remember?"

"Absolutely," I say.

"Do you want to borrow my crayon?" she asks. "It's magic and draws all by itself."

"Sure," I say, putting it in my pocket. "Thanks."

"Bye," she says in a singsong voice, and walks backward, waving to me, all the way to her driveway.

Turning back to the house, I notice the Dark Lady roses, which Grams planted when I was a baby, blooming by the front door. I lean into their perfume and decide to bring this deep red sweetness into the house. I'll cut some to take to Grams, too.

I ferret out Grams's favorite vase, arrange the Dark Ladies, and sprinkle shells around the base like Grams used to do.

Once I place the scarlet roses on the porch, I feel like being out here, too. I grab my journal and start writing. A poem takes shape almost immediately, my words flowing like a sketch when it's going well.

RESCUE

I was covered
in earth and leaves
when the white-throated sparrow inside me
sang,
reminding me of the tops of trees,
and who I am when I stand up.

So I push
hard
off the ground
and run
into my own arms.

The whoosh of words surges energy through me. I take off for Whitcomb Hill, Grams's and my favorite place when we need to think or just be. I stride fast and hard and arrive up top sweaty and out of breath. Then I hunker down, leaning into the warmth of our rock, Victoria Rose; breathe in the cleansing air; and watch the sun-shimmered waters of Puget Sound far below.

The bright afternoon light is just fading into the gentler tones of early evening when a smattering of ideas for a collage begin to take shape. And more thrilling than that, I feel my fingers twitch. I feel the creature that soars within me when I'm sliding into the place where I create.

When I bound in the door, Dad's in the kitchen.

"I want to make something!" I shout, exhilarated to be feeling like this again.

Dad points to a pot on the stove with a long wooden spoon. "I've already started making dinner," he says.

"Not dinner—art!" I say. "I think I'm getting it back."

"Then I'd better hold dinner until you're done."

"That'd be great. Thanks!"

"Run like the wind," he replies, just like Grams used to.

I take the steps two at a time. Upstairs, I pull out a pile of old Chagall calendars that have been stuffed under my bed forever. I flip through the months and years, cutting out pictures until the floor is strewn with scraps of calendar.

I gather up the reds, turquoises, and yellows; the dancers, fliers, players, and dreamers, and spread them all over my bed. I choose a girl riding a rooster to tape up over my dresser. I plaster all the pictures of people playing violins together, like they're jamming on the outside of my closet. A couple kissing as they fly out a window flies above my real window. A naked couple lying in a vase of lilacs goes on the ceiling, and on the back of the door a girl with long white hair floats beside a red moon and the Eiffel Tower. I cut, rip, and paste until Chagall's wildness is all over my room.

Then I take glue and a stiff brush and begin a huge collage on a giant piece of poster board with the rest of the snippets. I paint my own designs in between Chagall's. When I'm done, I have this enormous Marc Chagall–and–Taylor Rose Wickham collaboration.

I fling myself on my bed and close my eyes. Grams appears inside my head, wearing a mint green gown with a rose-petal shawl. She flies spirals around my room and then lands beside me on the bed. The bed turns into a sailboat on a magenta sea with an azure-striped sail. All around us marigold yellow and poppy red birds are singing, and Grams spreads her wings, saying what she always says. "Take sweetness into your life. Embrace what you love."

After playing in this vision for a while, I sit up and gaze at all the color and life all over the place.

"Look at this!" I say to Mai Ling, who's propped up on my pillow, holding Halle's purple crayon. "My room is stunning. I love it in here! Dad," I call. "Come on up and see what I've done!"

34

I WAKE UP FEELING SO GREAT that I run down to the beach and watch the sun rise. Sitting in the cool and quiet of the morning, watching birds fish and the sun sparkle the water, I feel happiness rise inside me.

Hours later, my growling stomach sends me home. I see Mr. Matheson standing on our front stoop. He's leaning way over, messing with something.

"Hi," I say coming up from behind him.

"I brought these over for you, Taylor girl."

"You brought me thorns?" I'm not sure if I'm supposed to know what I'm looking at. They just look like thorny sticks to me.

"They're prickly, all right, but sweet in the summer. These are raspberry canes from my garden. And here's how to plant them," he adds, handing me an envelope. "These are from the same plants that your grandma has been picking from. We tried once to plant some in your yard, but they didn't have enough sun. That was good by me—I liked any excuse to have Alessa stop by." He winks at me and I smile. "But now that they took the silver maple out, you'll have plenty of sun. They'll turn into raspberry bushes, and in a few more summers you'll have baskets of berries. Your grandma has a little berry basket that lets the raspberries land soft. It's at my place right now, but you can come and collect it sometime. Alessa would be real happy to know she finally has my berries growing in her yard."

What a sweet man. I love how he talks so naturally about Grams. Seeing him here is like old times. "Mr. Matheson's here," Grams would say happily as I came in from school. Being with him makes me remember the way Grams would burst through the door, calling us in for lemonade. She always did or said the delightful thing, and that's what she'd do on this hot day.

"Mr. Matheson, would you like to come in for some lemonade?" I ask.

"Why yes, that would be nice."

As I lead him into the kitchen, I feel shy, not sure what we'll talk about. Grams was always the one to keep conversations going. He pulls out a chair and sits down at the kitchen table, gently touching the petals of the roses as I bring the pitcher over.

"Your grandma's as sweet and prickly as raspberries and roses," he says, picking up the lemonade glass I've placed in front of him. "Knowing her has given me more interesting days than I can tell you. I just have to think of some funny thing she's done or said and I get myself laughing."

"She used to make me laugh all the time, too."

"Still does for me," he says.

"I like the way you think of Grams the way she was. I have a hard time doing that."

"It's easy and hard for me, too," he says. "I just hold on to her as best I can. She may not know it's me anymore, but I know it's her."

"Mr. Matheson, does Grams know someone named Jimmy?" I ask suddenly.

"Yes," he says in a quiet voice. "She certainly does. That's me."

"*You?*"

"I am the fortunate one, yes," he says. "I'm her second Jimmy."

"Her *second* Jimmy?"

"Her first Jimmy went off to war and never came back,

183

and then she married your grandfather. I came along just a moment too late, but after your grandfather and my Violet passed on—well, Alessa and I have kept each other shined up."

"So *you're* Jimmy?" I say. "The Jimmy who Grams always waits for? The one who brings her roses and raspberries?"

"I'm both now," he says. "Some days I'm her first Jimmy, and I bring her roses. Some days I'm me, the one who brings raspberries."

"So Jimmy *does* come!" I say.

"Yes, he does," he says.

We sit silently for a long time. I never thought of Grams needing anyone but Dad and me.

"Yes, he most certainly does," he says slowly. "She's my dearest."

"Mine, too," I say. "And thanks for the raspberry plants."

"Alessa loves sweet and tart. Raspberries are all of that. Get those planted and you'll have sweet things to look forward to. Not that I'd mind if you came picking at my place, too."

"Aren't you sad or mad or *anything* about Grams being sick?"

Mr. Matheson puts down his glass, rubs his chin, and lays a hand on my shoulder.

"I'm all those things, honey," he says. "I miss her all day long and in the middle of the night, when I wouldn't have seen her anyway. But it doesn't mean I forget who your grandma is. She wants us picking raspberries, not pitching rocks or stopping in our tracks."

Mr. Matheson pats my arm and then uses it for support as he pushes himself up. He takes his glass to the sink, washes it, removes the towel from the hook under the sink, and dries it. Then he puts the glass in the cupboard, right where it belongs.

"Well, I'd best be going," he says.

"Thanks for the raspberry bushes," I say again. "And the instructions. I'll plant them right away."

"They'll like that," he says. "Thanks for the lemonade."

"It's Grams's recipe," I say.

"It tastes just as good as she ever made it. Maybe better. I'll enjoy telling Alessa we had lemonade together. She'll like that."

"She hardly ever knows it's me when I go," I say, feeling confused. "Does she know it's you?"

"Doesn't matter, honey," he says. "I tell her anyway."

"Thanks, Mr. Matheson."

"My pleasure," he says. "And please call me James, dear."

Then he's out the front door, down the steps, and gone.

Later in the day, when it's cooler, I carry a trowel and the raspberry sticks, in the moist rags Mr. Matheson has them wrapped up in, out to the garden.

"Look at you out here," says Dad, when he arrives home. "What are those things?"

"Raspberry bushes."

"Let me get changed and I'll come out and help you finish up," he says.

When he returns, he kneels down and helps me plant the last of the bushes around the stump of the silver maple. It feels great to be out here with Dad planting these raspberries.

Dad speaks first. "Raspberries, eh?"

"Yes," I say. "They're from James Matheson."

"Well," says Dad. "That's perfect."

"Why?"

"Because Grams loves him," says Dad. "And she loves raspberries."

"And us," I say.

"And us," he repeats.

"Hey, Dad," I say. "I think I do want to use Grams's room—as my art studio."

"Good," he says. "She'd like that."

35

I GET UP EARLY THE NEXT MORNING, make tea, pour it into Grams's favorite blue flowered mug, and take it out to the porch. A few minutes later Dad comes out, carrying his coffee and holding something behind his back. He joins me on the porch steps.

"Good morning," he says, and scratches my head.

"Hi, Dad. Find any lice?"

"I've been thinking about you a lot lately," he says, sitting beside me.

"Yeah?" I say with a smile.

"Yes. Grams gave you as many pieces of your mom as she could—I left that to her. But you've helped me realize that's not right. I appreciate the way you've encouraged me to open up, to let the good memories back in."

"It's been hard for me to do that with Grams, the way she is now," I say. "So I guess I understand a little bit better."

Dad shifts and brings out a lavender drawstring bag from behind his back. "Your mom wanted you to have this someday," he says, placing it gently on my lap.

Tiny silver hearts dangle from the ends of the drawstrings and periwinkle stars from the bottom of the velvet bag. On the side of the bag is an embroidered purple heart with my initials, T.R.W., and my mother's, L.E.W., on it. It feels like all the little hairs on my arms are standing up, and my stomach is zinging like I'm about to leap off a high dive or tell a guy I love him.

Inside the bag is a beautiful journal. On its cover is a replica of *The Birthday*, one of my favorite Chagall paintings.

"I'd forgotten Lee chose Chagall," he says.

"I can't *believe* she chose Chagall."

On the inside of the front cover is a message to me.

For Taylor, my sweet little girl.
I love you.
XOXOXOX
Mom

I feel like Dorothy must've felt when the Good Witch touched her with a wand and everything around her shimmered. I reread the *I love you* part over and over.

"How could she know me well enough to love me?" I ask Dad, afraid that my mom had just been writing words.

"She carried you inside of her for nine months and loved you every moment of that time. She listened to your heart and talked to you. She sang to you, read you poems, and danced you around our living room. And then she had seven months of holding you in her arms, touching and loving you as you nuzzled at her breast."

My body heaves like waves crashing against rocks, and then I cry so hard I have to let go of the book. When Dad slides over and puts his arm around my shoulder, I snuggle into that safe harbor until my sobbing stops. Then I pick up the journal and carefully turn the pages. I randomly stop at an entry dated three months before I was born.

*To my daughter—my first time to write or use these words—
I thought I'd tell you a few little things about myself. Even
though I'm a woman, sometimes I feel like a little girl, wide-
eyed and playful. I'm in love with Max, your dad. I laugh,
cry, get angry and scared. I've always danced in the living
room when I'm alone, but now I dance with you inside me. I
already love you.*

This is the first time I've heard my mother's voice.

I slowly turn each page and discover flattened rose
petals, pressed green leaves from a cedar, a blue jay feather,
a cartoon, a pair of faded theater tickets, and an Emily
Dickinson poem. I turn to a page that has green and blue
smears, with a caption beside each one. *Dandelion,* says
one. *Clover leaf. Violet. Grass from the garden. Leaf from
silver maple.* She has swiped plants across the page to
make colors and designs with their juice.

After that is a page titled *Max. He's quiet and I'm loud,
but inside he's as loud as I am. He's a gift before it's opened,
and Christmas Eve, and a secret whispered in my ear. Such a
lovely man.*

She'd pasted in a picture of Dad smiling and holding
me as a baby in his arms.

"This is so sweet," I say quietly. "I've never seen this
one. I love the look on your face."

"Lee loved that picture," he says softly, bending over
for closer look and patting my shoulder. "She used to
have it tucked into the corner of her mirror."

One month before I was born she'd written: *I've been singing to you for over an hour. I read you poetry every day and play you beautiful music—Mozart's string quartets and Pavarotti singing Puccini are filling our house today. When you emerge, some things may seem familiar—my laugh, the smell of a rose. I'll keep this book a surprise until some day when you need a gift like this.*

I love you forever, Mom.

Mom! *My mother.*

There are no words for words. Sometimes they say a picture is worth a thousand of them, but all the pictures in the albums in the living room, even the beautiful one on Dad's dresser of Mom laughing with her arm around Grams, can't give me my mother as her words do. The ink in this journal has kept her heart beating in the world long after she left it.

While I continue turning the pages, a photograph of my mom and dad falls out of the book. Dad's pushing Mom on the swing that used to hang from the silver maple, there's a sprinkler shooting water at them, and they're both laughing.

I hear a choking noise and look up to see Dad crying. His hands are limp over his knees, and his head is hanging down, sagging onto his chest. He looks like someone who thinks he might faint and is trying to get the blood to rush to his head, only he's shaking and I see tears spattering his shoes. I feel my hands go cold, because I've never seen Dad cry before and I don't know how to respond.

"Dad?" I say, as I ease the tilted coffee cup out of his hand.

I'm scared to see him like this. And I'm also weirdly happy. I'm scared because Dad never cries. I'm happy because he is, finally.

"Dad," I say again, slipping my arm around his shoulders.

He lifts his face, and it's like watching a wall of ice melt. As if his real face is being released from a block of marble by some invisible sculptor. Almost as if all these years he's worn a mask of himself and now his real face is emerging. He looks at me with his new sweet face, and I'm so touched by his open look that I can't remember words.

36

"AND SHE USED TO PILFER flowers from other people's gardens," says Dad at breakfast the next day.

I eat up everything Dad tells me, hungry to hear every particle of my mom's life. Dad's stories are filling up the empty pockets in my soul that I've carried around for years. And I love how his face looks in this new soft place.

Later on, as we're cleaning up the breakfast dishes, I announce, "I'm going to buy Grams a present today."

"Great idea," he says. "What are you thinking of getting?"

"Well," I respond, "I know she doesn't need anything, but I have a need to give her something."

Dad nods his head and wraps an arm around me. "I'm going to do some shopping of my own—groceries," he says. "Want anything special?"

"Yes," I say, feeling extremely happy. "Bring home *lots* of special things!"

I wander downtown to look in the shops for something to get Grams. The first thing I think of is roses, so I wander into the florist's. In the back of the shop I find a wooden rack with tiny bottles, each containing the scent of a flower. One has a silver rose on its side. I open it, and the strong fragrance causes me to close my eyes as I picture Grams pulling me outside to smell the first summer rose last June. Standing together in the early morning, our bare toes wet from the dew, welcoming the first rose, she'd said, "After you, my dear!" and I let the smell of that one red rose fill me up. "Don't sniff out all the smell," she'd said, laughing. "Leave some for me."

I buy the rose oil for Grams and tuck it into my pocket.

When I walk out of the store, I see Mindy, hanging out with Beth Lindgrin and Luke Masterson, two of her high school buddies.

"Hey, Taylor," says Mindy.

"What's up?" I answer.

"Wren's pregnant," says Beth, in one of those whispers everyone within a block can hear.

"You're kidding," I say. I've never seen Wren even talk to a guy.

"Yup," says Beth.

"Trapped by fertile eggs," quips Luke, as Beth swats his shoulder.

"Whoever he is, *his* life'll go on the same," says Mindy fiercely. "No matter what *she* does, she's *screwed*. She either has her baby or she has it killed. She's wrecked either way."

"Screwed by the ultimate wrecking balls!" says Luke, delighted by his own wit.

"I'm getting a soda," declares Beth, pushing Luke so hard that he nearly topples over. "Come on, lamebrain. How about you, Mindy?"

"I'm going to hang with Taylor for a minute," says Mindy.

I'm glad she says this.

"Weird about Wren, huh?" says Mindy. She looks at me for a moment as she absently rubs her stomach, and then suddenly looks incredibly sad. And in that instant, I just know: Mindy's been pregnant. I bet it happened last summer, when I was away in Europe. No wonder she didn't care about anything in *my* life. She must've been through hell.

"I can't even look after myself yet," I say to her quietly. "I'd never be able to make it smooth for a kid."

"Same," says Mindy.

"I'm not finished giving birth to me," I continue.

"How could I do it for someone else? I don't blame anyone who'd choose not to have a baby."

"Really?" says Mindy, looking up.

"Really," I say. "We're too young to have babies."

Mindy starts crying, and I put my arm around her and pat her hair. She leans against my shoulder.

"It must be a horror to get pregnant by accident," I say.

"Yeah," says Mindy. "Like falling into a nightmare you can't wake up from or make any better. I know someone who's going to cry on the anniversary of her baby's—of her abortion."

It's weird how you can keep looking at a face without realizing that you've stopped seeing it. Now I see that Mindy has changed; she no longer has that confident take-on-the-world look. There's sadness in her eyes, as if she hasn't truly laughed in a long time.

"She even named her baby before it died," continues Mindy.

"What was the baby's name?" I ask.

"Blaire," she says, sobbing. "A month old this June." She can't talk anymore for crying.

"Oh, Mindy!" I say, wrapping my arms around her.

How did I not notice the way her face has changed? *This was my best friend.*

I imagine a little baby named Blaire, her bright eyes smiling and her little hands reaching out to touch some new wonder in her new world. My shoulders shiver, but I hold Mindy till she stops crying.

"Has this year sucked, or *what?*" I say.

Mindy wipes her eyes and blows her nose. "You got that right."

Beth and Luke stroll back toward us carrying sodas and chips.

"What is it, Mins?" asks Beth, stepping between Mindy and me as though I was trying to steal her friend away.

"PMS," says Mindy.

"Poor baby," says Beth, as she pats Mindy's arm. "Can I get you something?"

I back away to give Beth space. "I'm going to take off," I say. "See you."

Mindy gives me a quick hug and whispers, "Don't tell anyone, OK?"

"No problem," I say.

I'm supremely weirded out at how people can appear so solid and self-sufficient while they're melting away and filling with tears.

I wander to the beach, thinking about Mindy. I find a place that's off to the side where I can lie perfectly still and let the sun warm me while I think. I'm settling in when Conlin, Mike's best friend, comes over and starts gaping at my body as if perhaps, if he stares hard enough, my tank top will fall off.

"You're a beautiful creature," he says, touching my arm lightly. Apparently, he and Mike took the same correspondence course on pukey pickup lines.

I shift so his hand can't reach me. "Don't touch me," I

say. "Not now, not ever. You want a beautiful creature, go to the zoo."

"I hear you're a good time."

"I am," I say. "However, not for the likes of you, or for your ape friend who I knocked on his butt. Now make like a slug and slime off."

He shrugs and walks away, dragging his feet along the sand.

I sit up to watch a little kid in bright red boots with a yellow-and-red-striped sand pail, who's splashing in and out of the water.

I flop down again and let the whoosh of the waves lull me. I'm slipping into a dream of blue when I feel the top of my head grow extra warm and feel a light pressure. Bears is lying down on the sand, too, his head touching mine and his feet shooting away. If we were a clock, we'd be three o'clock.

"What's up, Lifeguard Boy?" I say.

"An entire town of safe swimmers," he says, yawning. "There's no excitement on this beach today."

"Isn't that supposed to be a good thing?" I ask, laughing.

"I was just going to ask if you'd fake a struggle, so I'd get a chance to use one of our new rescue boards."

"Sorry, there's no struggle in me today," I say. "I'm taking a break from drowning. I'm just going to float safely here on this soft sand."

I roll over to face Bears, he does the same, and we're eye to eye. Staring at him like this makes me feel shimmery, like I've turned into particles of dancing dust in a shaft of light.

"Did you put on sunscreen?" he asks.

"Aren't you taking this life-guarding thing a little over the top?" I say.

He sits up and snaps open a bottle of suntan lotion, spreading a thin white line down one of his fingers. Then he reaches over and touches my warm back with the cool, moist tip of his finger and begins to trace designs.

"I'm writing, *You are beautiful*," he says.

I luxuriate in the sound of his voice and the feel of his finger, even though I wish he were writing something else. After Mike and Conlin, the "beautiful" line seems more like a warning than words to sink into.

"Hey, T," he whispers in my ear, and I feel a little shiver of anticipation run through me. I feel like he's closer to kissing me than he's ever been, and I'm already closing my eyes.

"Do you want to come into the equipment shed with me?" he says.

"What?" I say, confused.

"The equipment shed is private," he says. "We could have it all to ourselves."

Great! He finally wants to kiss me, but he wants to do it in a *closet!* And just because he's writing *You are beautiful* does not mean I'll do whatever he wants.

"Forget it!" I shout, leaping up. "*Beautiful* will get you nowhere, and I'm not a Closet Girl!"

I run off past the little kid in the red boots, down the beach, and head out to the rocks. As I scramble up to the very top, I turn and see Bears behind me, and I explode like a firecracker. "Stop *following* me!"

"What just happened?" Bears yells back. "What the hell is wrong?"

I turn my back to him, ashamed that I've let my anger at Mike spill over onto Bears. When I turn around, he's gone.

At home I shuffle through a stack of CDs, find Dad's copy of Stravinsky's *Firebird,* and slam it into the machine. I turn up the volume like I'm turning the wheel of my bike hard around a tight corner. I want it loud enough to create wind whipping through the house, blowing away the clutter of thoughts and feelings I've let pile up inside me. I sit hugging my knees. When the music ends, there are tears all down my legs.

37

DAD FINDS ME ON THE FLOOR next to a speaker, red-eyed and snuffling into a Kleenex.

"What's up?" he says. "Are you down about Grams?"

It'd be so easy just to nod yes, to keep him out. "No," I say, wiping stray tears off my cheek. "Bears and I had a fight."

"Ah," says Dad.

"He wanted to take me to the lifeguard closet to make out. And he said I'm beautiful."

"What a jerk!" says Dad, laughing.

"No, Dad," I say. "Telling me I'm beautiful is a line that guys drop just so they can get some action." I'm not sure I've ever said anything like this to Dad before.

Dad looks startled for a second. Then he laughs. "You're as smart-mouthed as your mother was! Suspicion runs in your veins."

"What's that supposed to mean?"

"The first time I spoke to your mother, I asked her for help with a science lab. She said she'd help me with the work, but she wouldn't go out with me. I'd have to ask her outright, some other time, if I wanted a date."

"Why'd she think you wanted to ask her out?" I ask, so hungry for stories about Mom that I put Bears and me on hold for a moment.

"Because that *is* what I wanted. Your mom was pretty and smart, and boys figured out ways to be near her all the time. She wanted me to come at her straight, not sideways. And she was sensitive about people just liking her because she was pretty instead of for who she was."

"Yeah, well—me, too," I say.

"So what do you think Bears wants from you? You must think it's really bad, to make you angry at him for wanting it," says Dad. "Do you like him in a romantic way?"

"Maybe," I say, feeling like an idiot, because I realize that I do like Bears, romantically and every which way.

"Do you have a fear of closets?" asks Dad with a chuckle.

"No."

"Well, then, what's your problem? You *are* beautiful, honey," says Dad. "Inside and out. Grams knew that. I know that. And, apparently Bears does, too. The only other relevant question that I can think of is, Have you eaten?" Dad can finish a subject before it's even started.

"I'm not hungry," I say. "I'm stupid."

"Aren't we all," says Dad, and he leaves the room humming *The Lover's Waltz*. Humming! Just when I think I know someone, I don't know him at all.

I guess Bears is thinking the same thing about me right now.

"Stupid," I say again. "*Unbelievably* dumb!"

I've just been a jerk to a person I like and who likes me. Grams always loved me for myself, no matter how stupid I was acting. Next time I visit Grams, I'm going to make sure I see more than just her outsides. I've been treating her like a bunch of skin-and-bone parts lumped in a chair instead of who she truly is. James Matheson knows that Alessa Rose is still a dancing girl.

I'd love to rewind the day, gracefully following Bears into that shed, running my hands up under his lifeguard shirt and kissing him soft and hard, deep and long, laughing, licking the salt off his chest and whispering words that make him weak.

It's almost midnight when a thought sends me running

to the garage, where I find an old Maxwell House coffee can filled with a jumble of colored sidewalk chalk.

I rush over to Bears's house carrying the can of chalk, the images of what I'm about to do dancing in my mind. By the light of a three-quarter moon and the arc of the streetlight, I crouch on Bears's driveway. I draw a girl and a boy holding hands, flying out a window toward the ocean, with a crow swooping under them, holding a basket of raspberries in its beak. I make a circle of girls playing violins and a boy strumming a guitar. I draw swirls of fuchsia, sweeping stripes of apricot, spirals of violet and sea green, saffron streamers, rainbow ribbons, a patch of sapphire blue forget-me-nots, amber children flying through cobalt stars, a cherry red swing holding two people, one wearing periwinkle pumps and the other in turquoise sneakers; olive sandwiches with indigo dots, crimson cleome with midnight blue wings, gold bells, and a long stretch of beach strewn with sea glass, shells, and oranges. I create violet, burgundy, and magenta silver-maple leaves fluttering off their branches and filling up the driveway.

I draw until there's no more chalk and there's no more sidewalk or driveway showing around Bears's house. The last thing I draw is a porch swing in a postcard frame, and on the postcard I write *BEARS, I'm sorry! T.*

I'm breathing hard and realize that I'm back in The Place, the zone where art and ideas, like a raging fire, blaze through me and onto my canvases. This is the best piece I've done in my entire life, and I don't care that it's going to be washed away when it rains. I'm back and there'll be more, plenty more.

Light is seeping into the sky as I slip beneath my moon-and-stars comforter, and the first bird of the morning begins to sing. As I pull my pillow into my arms and begin to drift asleep, I happily realize, *I'm finally awake.*

38

I OPEN MY EYES and everything's fresh. I gave the most magnificent gift to Bears, and as I drew, one of my very own wishes came true. I'm back in myself, only new.

I watch as the wind picks up and raindrops begin to pound onto the porch roof. My masterpiece is about to vanish into a river of rain.

I pull on my purple T-shirt and ripped jeans, head downstairs, and step out into the storm. It feels cool and alive on my skin. Drops pelt my head and bounce off my eyelids. My eyelashes collect rain until I can barely see.

I'm truly alive, and I dance in the rain, celebrating. I remember Grams used to swear rainwater is great for hair, so I dash into the house, dripping and sliding over the kitchen floor, and grab some shampoo—biodegradable—from the hall cupboard.

Out in the garden I pour shampoo on my head, lean back, close my eyes, and feel the raindrops smacking my face. I sense a presence and squint to see Bears. He grabs me and twirls me around in the rain.

"You did it!" he shouts, still whirling.

I'm dizzy and laughing when he eventually puts me down.

"It's really, really good, T. It's incredible."

"You saw it!" I say.

"Yes! It's the best work you've ever done, and I'm blown away that you made it for me. Thanks."

"You're welcome. Let's celebrate!"

"You're amazing," he says.

"Thank you, thank you, thank you!" I say, looking back at him through the rain. "Here." I smile wide and hand him the shampoo bottle. "Join the party."

He pours the shampoo onto my head instead of his own.

"I meant for you!" I say, laughing.

He ignores me, placing his hands on my head, sliding the shampoo through my hair, and pulling strands gently through his fingers. His touch is so delicate and sure, I feel as if I'm a mandolin being played. My skin sings and my breath melts into a melody wafting in and out. And then he traces designs down my arms, along my back, my neck, and my body. I want to twine around Bears like ivy on a trellis or perhaps a climbing rose.

"You're done," says Bears.

I don't move, but stand silent and still as the rain beats upon my head.

"Hey," says Bears, kissing me lightly on my cheek.

"I'm a rose," I say, slowly opening my eyes.

Bears is one breath away. He flicks suds from his fingers onto my shirt. I grab lather out of my hair and fling it at him as he grabs my arms. I slip away and he chases after me. We skid around on the grass, tussling and tossing suds. When he grasps my arms again, I lean in instead of away, and we're riveted on each other's eyes.

I reach out and touch his hair, he pulls me into him, and maybe for a moment we actually melt together. My body vibrates, I'm silver and gold. If I kiss him now it'll be like kissing a whole summer's day—all the roses and sweetness I've longed to taste for a long, long time.

Grams always said, If a door or even the crack of a window opens, at least take a peek. So I lean in and kiss those soft, familiar, completely new lips. And he tenderly kisses me back until I'm violet wings in a sea green sky. I want to stay wings and sky for a *long* time, but our lips sort of pop apart and here we are again. And here we aren't. I'm not sure who is left standing sizzling in the rain. Thunder rumbles.

"Hey," I say.

"Mmmm," he says.

"I'll sketch you something new," I say.

"Great! And I won't invite you into a closet again," he says.

I laugh.

"Maybe you'll use your new sable brush," he adds.

"From you?" I start to ask, and then it's not a question. "Of course you! Thank you."

And we're kissing again with rain dripping down our foreheads and running into our mouths. I'm kissing his lips and kissing the rain and everything feels new.

I try phoning Ebbie again, and this time she's there.

"Ebbs!" I shout into the receiver. "I chalked a sidewalk and made a collage. I kissed Bears in the rain. And I'm eating things!"

Ebbie's laughter turns into cheers. "You're on a roll, girl," she says.

"I know it! And get this—the big news flash is that Dad and I actually buy groceries like normal people, *and* he's learned how to cook!"

"How great is that!"

"Totally great. Are you having a blast?" I ask.

"Total," she says. "Other worlds exist. There are places beyond Whidbey."

"I'm glad we sent someone off-island to find out."

"Hey, I'm so happy you're back in the groove, Ant Leader."

"I know it. I feel as though I've been freed from the clutches of dull—I have my life back, literally! OK, now tell me about you. Are you eating things, too?"

"I'm afraid I've been civilized, Taylor."

"No!" I shout into the phone. "Was it painful? Maybe it's reversible. Stay in your room, lock your door, and I'll

catch the next ferry and perform an intervention. How did they get you?"

"They've been forcing me to have afternoon tea *every day* since I got here."

"I'm on my way! In the meantime, do not extend your baby finger, touch a teacup, or take another sip. Swear, spit, and scratch your armpits to reverse the effects."

"It may be too late, T," says Ebbie in a weak and trembly voice.

"Those evil Canadians!" I say dramatically.

"Tea is actually cool, Antennae Girl. It's like having grown-up recess in the middle of the day. They stop, sit, sip, and munch delectables. It's a great concept."

"Let's do it when you get back," I say.

"You got it. Tea with T."

"Hey, I miss you, Ebb. It's so great to hear your wacko voice."

"I miss you, too! How's Grams?"

"Not great," I say. "But I'm a better visitor. I'm no longer an asshole."

Ebbie laughs again and then her voice gets soft. "You had a crappy year. Hey, did you get my postcard?"

"Yes."

"Did you hate it?"

"Yup. It's displayed on my mirror."

"Great. Hey, Taylor, I've got to run. Take care," she says.

"Take care of you, and don't go getting polite or saying *eh*," I say back, and hang up happy.

39

THE NEXT DAY WHEN I wake up, my lips still feel warm from yesterday's kisses. I lean on my windowsill, looking over at Bears's house and wishing I could fly, like one of Chagall's floating people, through the air and into his window.

But I shift from these lovely feelings into project mode. Today's the day I've set aside to surprise Grams, the day she's going to get her three-roses-to-every-slice birthday cake. I've helped her make my birthday cake every year since I was three, so I know how to make it right.

The whole house is cheering to have the smell of baking drifting through its rooms again.

"This smells great!" says Dad, as he pokes his head into the kitchen. I start attacking the wonderful mess, which has caused the sink to disappear under a mountain of sticky bowls and pans.

When the cake is cool, I take out Grams's old silver-colored icing tube with the tiny nozzles for delicate designs. I fill up the tube, roll up my sleeves, and start to swirl. When I'm finished, there's not a smooth piece of icing left on the top of the cake. Instead of three roses for every slice, it's *all* roses.

"Well, somebody has her creative juices flowing again," says Dad, his face beaming. "This is truly a remarkable cake, Taylor Rose."

"I wish you could be there when I give it to her, Dad, but I'll bring a piece back for you."

"We'll go together tomorrow," he says, and squeezes my hand. "Who knows what you'll come up with by then."

I put the brush Bears gave me and seven tubes of paint into my backpack, lower the cake into a container, and put the rose-scented bottle in my jacket pocket, along with Grams's hairbrush. Dad hugs me, and I take off for the Golden Edges and Grams.

She's lying in her bed instead of sitting in her chair. "Grams," I say, concerned. "Are you OK?"

She just keeps staring into space, an occasional blink her only sign of life. I walk over to the bed and show her the cake. A small smile creases her wrinkled face as she reaches for it.

"We should all get roses," I say.

I set the cake down beside her, open the silver bottle of scent, and move it slowly back and forth under her nose. Then I take her hands in mine and gently rub the backs of her cold fingers. After I've warmed her hands, I begin to paint them. Over the wrinkles on her knuckles I paint tiny purple crescent moons and one gold star. On her palms I paint cerulean blue violins with wings, a magenta tulip along one ring finger, and an African violet on the other. I paint a bouquet of roses on the back of her right hand and a basket of ripe raspberries on the back of her left. I want to send the universe a thousand gifts of thanks for this chance to touch Grams again.

When I'm finished, she lifts her hands, turning them all around, as though she is looking at an exotic work of art.

"I'm going to be OK, Grams," I say. "I don't think I'll ever have another day so perfectly fine as when you were home, but I'm doing OK. And guess what? Bears and I had a cool day yesterday. He washed my hair in the rain, and we kissed."

Grams's lips move, but I can't hear what she's saying, not even when I lean down and put my ear only an inch from her mouth. And then I become overwhelmed by the sadness of the moment and start crying so hard I can't even talk.

When I finally quiet down, I remember her hairbrush. I take it out and start to softly brush her hair.

"Grams," I say, "I found your journal. I hope it's OK that I read it. I love what you wrote."

I don't know if she understands or not, but she squeezes my hand, and I squeeze hers back. Her lips move again. I still can't hear her, so I bend down even closer, my earlobe brushing against her lips. Her breath tickles, but I can't hear any words. Instead, I hear her voice inside my head. *I love you, Taylor Rose.*

And then I just wrap my arms around her and hold her, hoping that all my love for her will soak into her bones. I guess love must soak into me, too, because when I stop hugging her, her eyes are no longer focused on me, but I don't run away. I don't want to do that anymore.

I set her hairbrush down next to her bed. Then I kiss her bewildered cheeks, and stroke her fingers warm again, and touch her sweet lips with a kiss.

"Bye, Grams. I love you."

40

AS WE WALK ALONG THE BEACH the next day, I slip my hand into Bears's and tell him about Grams and the cake of roses, and about my call to Ebbie. After he goes on duty, I wander along the shore, stopping from time to time to draw: rock formations jutting out at low tide, a gathering of sanderlings eating bugs up and down the shoreline. I find an egret silently fishing in a quiet cove, and I sit down and leisurely sketch it. I know how much Dad likes these graceful birds, so I'll work from the sketch and surprise him with a painting.

When I get home, the answering machine is blinking like it has a pulse. Hoping it's Bears, I push the button and pick up a pencil.

"This is Eileen Lo, the head nurse at the Golden Edges. Mrs. Wickham is not doing well. A family member should arrange to get here as soon as—"

I freeze, then leap up and bang around the kitchen like a sparrow trapped in a shoebox. I call Dad at the office, but he's already gone. I start to call Bears, but remember he's on his way to a Mariners game. What the hell am I supposed to do now! I'm afraid to face what might be waiting for me at the Golden Edges, afraid that Grams's frail body is even weaker and more withered than it was yesterday.

But then I calm myself down. I know that her old bones and skin are not truly her. I know she's trapped and doesn't belong inside that failing mind. Grams is bare toes running through sprinklers, across sand, into ocean waves. She's hands snatching stars from the skies and turning them into fireflies. I feel the deep love that Grams has always wrapped me in, and I know the spirit that has lived behind those now dull eyes. I realize that I urgently want to be with her.

As I'm running out the door, I meet Mindy walking up our path. "Taylor, I'm so sorry."

"I don't really have the time right now, Min. I've got to get to Grams."

Mindy grabs my arms. "Don't you *know*, Taylor?" she says, her voice thin and starting to crack.

"Know?"

"She died, Taylor. Not quite an hour ago. I was there visiting my aunt Min. That's why I was coming here."

"Oh, no," I whisper, and crumple into Mindy's arms.

41

WHEN THE WORD "DIED" shot out of Mindy's mouth, I felt a jolt, as if the word had pierced my heart. One four-letter word and *snap,* Grams is gone.

"Thanks, Mindy," I say, pulling away and swiping my hand over my eyes. "There's something I need to do. I'll be OK."

I turn back to the house. I need to be alone to say my last goodbyes to Grams. There's a letter waiting for me in my top drawer that Grams wrote for this day. I slip upstairs to get it. Clutching the envelope, I walk up Whitcomb Hill as if I'm being slowly reeled to the top.

I sit with my back against Victoria Rose and cry until my eyes run dry, and then I'm ready to read what Grams has written to me.

For Taylor Rose, after I'm gone and it's time to let go.

My dear Taylor Rose,

We've been saying this poem together since you were three years old. I've changed the title and the way it ends. Hold on to it now, dear.
I love you.

Grams

UNWRAP ME

Christmas morning,
holding the first present.
She lifts her arms to stars, sky,
top of tall pine.
Shouts,
"Let it out!"

When you see me small in these bones, skin,
lift your arms to stars, shout,
"Let her out!"

Grams's words ring true in my heart. I imagine dying as a letting go, like releasing a balloon and watching it soar high above the tallest trees. I wonder if that's what it's like when you leave your body behind.

I lean into Victoria Rose, still warm from the day's sun, remembering how Grams and I celebrated my mom on this hill, and thinking that now I'm here to do the same for Grams.

I celebrate the way this rose-loving woman greeted each day as if waking up was a present. Here's to the lady who tap-danced in stores, spun a cartwheel across Main Street, sang while she pumped her gas, and ran naked through our sprinkler to celebrate turning eighty years old. I cheer her zest for life.

Grams never stopped doing the things she loved.

While Grams rooted for me, for Chagall, and for every rose that bloomed, she cheered for herself, too.

She celebrated what she loved, and that's what I'm doing up here. I'm holding up Grams's life and applauding. I'm shouting from the top of the hill that Alessa Rose Wickham lived life to the fullest and graduated from this planet *with honors.*

And I'm going to do that, too.

"So, Grams," I whisper, twirling a long piece of grass, "I'll take care of your roses and gather in what I love, like raspberries in a basket. I'm going to sip the sweet juice out of each of my days on this old earth, just like you did. You won't catch me dying while I'm alive—I'm not going to die until I'm dead."

I want to make Grams's poem fly, like a Chagall painting. I raise "Unwrap Me" above my head, and a gust of wind gives it a moment's flight.

"I love you, Grams!" I shout up into the sky.

Grams used to say, "It takes a lot of living to love, and sometimes love's just plain peculiar!" I say it's paint and words and breath and everything strange and yes and all you have to do is dip in.

I scoop up Grams's poem, tuck it into my pocket, and start down the hill toward our house. A place of joy and sorrow. Thorns and blossoms. Roses and raspberries. Bitter and sweet. And a life crammed full of love.